Locket of Lies

Written by: A.J. Huebner

*For my husband, David, who encouraged
me to follow my dreams, and my boys,
Kenneth and Luke, who love me unconditionally.*

Chapter 1

It is strange to think that in less than twenty-four hours, I will be exiting school and pursuing my assigned trade. I didn't exactly spend much time training for it, considering there aren't many young women in this town who don't know how to sweep, wash, and serve others. Never mind that I am extremely athletic (mostly from years spent running from Aparthia Nation's Royal Guard when I stole clothing or food from the market) and not the ugliest girl my duty is to serve at the pleasure of the royal family, with minimal regard to my athletic and intellectual abilities.

I am an orphan, and because of that, I do not have a last name, something I am constantly reminded of. I can't even describe the amount of time I spent dreaming I was born in the F class, into a family who owned their own business and loved me for my own talents rather than my looks and ability to clean. All I know about my family is what is written in the orphanage records:

"Orphaned at two months. Parents killed in battles."

I wish I knew more, but no one likes to talk about the battles before King Rennin Adair took the throne. I suppose that time brings back painful memories for all classes involved, considering many families, including the royal family, lost family members, and friends.

King Rennin's own father died during the battles, leaving Rennin himself to finish the battles and reign over the last remaining nation. He had to rebuild and find a way for our nation to take control of the other two nations, Anniah and Allenthia, swiftly before either one of them found a way to rebuild themselves. In that haste to rebuild, much of the crucial bits of information involving our society were lost or scattered.

As a result, the only other piece of information in my file at Ms. Morrow's orphanage is my birthdate, of course. Thanks to that, the royal family knows I am turning seventeen today, which means I have now aged out of the orphanage and school all in the same day.

"Happy Birthday" to me.

At the end of each month, the Royal Adair family collects all of the newly turned seventeen year olds and sends them through choosing ceremonies that kick off the start of our trades. I'm still not certain why the ceremonies are referred to as choosing, considering the seventeen year olds don't do any of the picking. The only ones who have a choice and make any selections are the individuals the seventeen year olds will work under. We all know what our trades will be; we just don't necessarily know who our direct bosses will be, with the exception of the Royal Guard and those drafted into it. This particular month is special though. The Royal Adair family is in need of more companions and servants, so this month's draft will be sent to the Golden Palace.

The remainder of today will be spent packing my belongings and preparing myself for the choosing ceremony at the Golden Palace, which will take place tomorrow morning.

In my heart, I know that if my family were here today, I would be someone important who wouldn't be assigned to the cleaning trade. I can't say that I would be in the A or B classes, but likely the F or K classes. Unfortunately, that isn't how our society works. Because I do not have a last name and am an orphan, I am a part of the W class, which is comprised of all families with last names beginning with the letters W, X, Y, and Z. If you are an orphan like me, you are automatically placed in this class. The A class is only the Royal Adair family. The B class is composed of last names that begin with letters B, C, D, and E, which means they are assigned the most prominent trades, such as government officials and royal advisors. The F class consists of letters F through J and is generated by the business owners in our city. The K class, which involves last names K through N serve as the educators in the local schools. Class O is letters O through R and these families are automatically trained and drafted into the Royal Guard. Letters S through V are the working class and assistants. This leaves the W class, which is made up of the servants, maids, and orphans of the community.

Gender does not matter to society. You follow the trade you are born into.

Our fates are set for us the second we are born. As a result, we grow up knowing our professions and trades right from the beginning. For women, the only chance for us to escape our strict destinies is to marry men with higher last names, which rarely occurs. Most men try to marry up themselves and have too much pride to marry down. When couples wed, the pair automatically adopts the trade and class of the higher of the two.

It is an endless circle of just trying to survive here. We train and work at our assigned trades. If we don't follow suit, we are ousted and sent to live in the Battle Grounds, which is the area between our nation and the other two royal nations. In school, we were taught that this area is where the battles occurred, so there is no vegetation, food, or water. Everything is simply dead and decaying because of all of the bombs and weapons utilized by all nations involved in the battles. Of course, no one has visited that area and returned to tell of its progress or lack of in years, at least since the battles ended roughly seventeen years ago, right after I was born.

If we elect not to be ousted, we are given pills that suffocate and kill us within minutes. They call those pills Instant Death. One less mouth for the royal family to feed and worry about, I suppose.

"Elaine, are you even listening to me? For a girl who was born to take orders from others, you sure aren't a very good listener."

"Sorry, Mrs. Klint. I was mentally preparing for my first day of trade."

"Well, I hope for your sake and the sake of the Royal Adair family you listen more attentively to them."

"Yes, ma'am. I will."

I'm not even sure why I am still sitting in this cold classroom. Today is my last day. There is nothing more for me to learn, nor anything Mrs. Klint can say that will better prepare me for my trade assignment tomorrow.

Despite the fact that I knew as an orphan I would never be given a fair chance at a trade, I worked hard in school and am exiting holding the number one position in the girls' division.

They do not allow boys and girls to compete against each other, so they use different scales to score us. Women are meant to keep quiet, do what is asked of our trade, and listen to the men in our society. Somewhere down the line and further back than anyone cares to remember, men were deemed the more intelligent of the sexes. I just wish someone would let me compete against the boys in my class and show everyone what I can really do. Somehow, judging by the way Paul (number one of the boys' division) carries himself, I believe I could beat him and put him in his rightful place - behind me in the academic ranks.

He must have felt me looking at him because he turns his head and scoffs at me. We have never seen eye to eye on anything, so we aren't exactly best friends. In fact, he has many friends, unlike me. I have kept to myself over the years and tried not to engage with too many people. There isn't any point because most of us won't be able to interact with each other anymore once we begin our trades. I've never understood why people put time into forming relationships just to have them disappear when they turn seventeen. That is why I can count my friends on one hand.

The day drags on and no one even attempts to say goodbye's to anyone, even though a few of us will be leaving permanently today.

Finally, school is over for good. I feel a slight tinge of sadness, knowing I will never be within these walls again, but also excitement since I won't have to watch Paul smirk at me anymore when his rank as number one is posted on the board for all to see.

The sadness doesn't last long, though. Ms. Morrow is already heading up the steps to collect me and walk me back to the orphanage. She does this sometimes to make sure I don't have the chance to head into the market and steal food for myself. She really believes what she feeds me is enough and that pang of hunger I haven't been able to escape in about ten years is all in my head.

As I head towards Ms. Morrow, Paul catches me off guard and inserts himself directly in my path.

"Happy Birthday, Elaine."

Somehow, just the way he says this to me sends chills down my spine.

"How did you know today is my birthday?"

"Because I pay close attention to details and know more than you think I do. You aren't the only one who will get to begin your trade tomorrow, so will I. However, unlike the servant life you will lead, I get to train with the Royal Guard. Then, you will have to take orders from me."

That's right. Paul's last name is Richter, so he will be drafted first thing tomorrow morning.

"I will not be taking orders from you since I am certain you will be a disgrace to the Royal Guard and they will oust you before your first day of training ends."

"We'll see about that. Seeing as how I was ranked number one in our class, I am sure I will supersede others in the Royal Guard and rise in the ranks there quickly too. Then, I plan on finding myself a wife to settle down with so I can have my own servant. You'd be so lucky to end up with a strapping man like me. I doubt you will ever find a man to marry, let alone someone who can stand you."

Before I can retort, Paul lifts his already high chin and stomps off. I'm not even sure why he stopped me other than to rub in his rank and class more than he already has over the years. His digs don't bother me, but the way he thinks so highly of himself does. I don't believe I've ever met such an obnoxious being in my seventeen years in this nation. I hope I never have to cross paths with that idiot again.

I know I should feel some pity for him because as a soldier in the Royal Guard, he might have to give his life to protect the Royal Adair's one day; however, I just can't bring myself to have any pity for him at the moment. Must be because he's so condescending and certain. Instead, I feel bad for the misfortunate men who share the same trade as him since they will now be living and training with him.

"Elaine, stop your moping. Hold your chin up. The Royal Guard might see you and report your behavior to the royal family. We wouldn't want that to jeopardize your chances of getting a supreme position in the Golden Palace."

Poor Ms. Morrow is hoping I am pretty enough to be chosen as a companion for one of the royals instead of just a servant who cleans up after them.

A companion is still a servant, but tends directly to the needs of the royal family members and accompanies them everywhere they go. If I were to be selected as a companion, I would get better sleeping facilities and the opportunity to travel with the Royal Adair family, so there's that benefit. Otherwise, I simply cannot think of how being a companion could be better than cleaning silently without having to entertain anyone.

"Just a few more minutes until we are home. Pull yourself together, girl!"

"If I hold my chin up any higher, the Royal Guard will assume I am trying to meet their gazes and will strike me for sure."

"Oh, nonsense. Maybe if you did make eye contact, one of them might notice how pretty you are. Then, you would become one of their problems and not mine."

"I will not be your *problem* anymore once I leave for the palace in the morning."

It is at that moment Ms. Morrow grabs my shoulders and spins me around to face her. "Before we reach the orphanage, there is something I need to talk to you about."

Her eyes are so sincere and melancholy at this very

moment that I actually notice how green they are for the first time in years. Her years of worrying about so many children have aged her eyes and caused an excess of wrinkles. With all of the orphans running around the house, we never have time to talk just the two of us.

"You know how I told you the records I have for you just say your parents died in the battles?"

"Yes, what about it?"

"Well, I know more, but was told never to discuss it with you or anyone to keep us both safe."

"What are you talking about, Ms. Morrow?"

"It's about your parents and who you really are. Your parents…"

"Whatever conversation you gossiping women are having can wait until you are behind closed doors. Go back home before you expose the rest of society to your childish ways."

The Royal Guardsman ushers us home and doesn't give us the chance to finish our conversation. What could Ms. Morrow possibly know about my parents that she has been keeping from me all of these years? I feel so betrayed. All I have ever wanted was to know something about my parents, something Ms. Morrow could have provided me with long ago.

Once inside, two different Royal Guardsmen in pressed, white uniforms embellished with gold greet us. This only means one thing the Royal Adair family has sent them.

Chapter 2

"Miss Elaine, it has come to our attention that you are seventeen today. This means you must accompany us to your holding room where you will await the choosing ceremony in the morning."

Before I can begin to process what the Royal Guardsman has just told me, Ms. Morrow intervenes on my behalf. "Since when is it customary for the Royal Guard to escort seventeen year olds to their trades the day before the ceremony?"

"Since King Rennin commanded the Royal Guard to do so this year. It may not be customary, but new rules are enforced all the time for the good of our nation. It is not my duty to ask why, just like it is not your right to ask the same."

I don't understand why King Rennin has sent his soldiers to collect me, let alone the other seventeen year olds, but I do know that it would be unwise for me to put up any sort of fight. "I will pack my belongings and be on my way shortly."

"There is no need. You will be given sufficient supplies and uniforms upon your arrival. You are only allowed to bring one change of clothes for tonight."

As I quickly rummage through the few belongings I have, I hastily pack one change of clothes, then glance around my small bedroom, and realize I really do not have anything special to me that I would be tempted to take with me and hide in my belongings. I have lived here for seventeen years, and yet, not a single one of the items in this room matters to me. It is easier this way. If you don't care about something, you aren't upset when the Royal Guard searches your belongings for anything that might offend the royal family, which is then burned in a pile for all to witness. They do this occasionally when rumors surface of people threatening to challenge the power of the Royal Adair family.

I turn to look at my room one last time and realize just how small this bedroom I have lived in for years truly is.

Because I was the oldest in the house, I had my own room, but that didn't happen until almost twelve years of sharing a room with other girls in the house. At one point, there were three sets of bunk beds in here for six of us to share. Anytime one of us got sick, it wasn't long before the rest of us shared the same illness.

The memory of growing up as a child in this room is quickly interrupted by harsh whispering coming from another room. Just down the hall of the small building, I can hear Ms. Morrow and the men in the Royal Guard talking quickly as though they have something to discuss that they do not want me to hear.

"Does this change in procedure have anything to do with the rumors?"

"Ma'am, I do not know what you are referring to. It would be wise for you to hand over the girl and keep your suspicions to yourself."

"You know exactly what I'm referring to. There are rumors circulating that one of the newly turned seventeen year olds may be a prominent family member of one of the royal families we defeated during the battles. If these rumors are true, then King Rennin will have a new battle on his hands sometime soon."

"These rumors have no truth to them. You know as well as I do that all of the royal family members from the other two nations were killed. Since all of them died, the Royal Adair family was the only royal family left to rule."

"And yet, King Rennin has made a drastic changes to ceremonial procedures. He must be worried about something."

"Listen here, old woman, you are pushing your luck and I will not stand for your boldness!"

I know Ms. Morrow is about to be struck for asking such brazen questions, so I scurry down the narrow hallway. It doesn't take long for the pair to notice me.

When I walk into the main room, Ms. Morrow grabs my shoulders and briefly hesitates before she pulls me in for one last hug. I study her and can tell the man representing the Royal Guard put his whip back on his hip before the leather tip had a chance to touch Ms. Morrow. I make certain to position myself between the man and Ms. Morrow so there is no chance of him sneaking in a strike at the old woman.

With my choosing ceremony in the Golden Palace looming, the Royal Guard is not allowed to lay a hand on me. For royal servants and companions to arrive any more dirty or disheveled than we already are is frowned upon.

Then, it happens so quickly that I do not realize Ms. Morrow has shoved something in the waistband of my old pants until I am walking back through the same front doors I have spent years sneaking in and out of.

Before I reach the end of the graveled walkway leading up to the orphanage, Ms. Morrow chants from the main room, "Keep your chin up and do not be afraid to use your pretty face to your advantage."

I know she means well, but I do not believe my pretty face will get me very far. It hasn't helped me a single time in my life leading up to this point, so I do not see how it could now.

Once on the dark street, I grip the small item in my waistband, that suddenly feels so heavy, and try to avoid making any obvious movements that might trigger my treason to the Royal Guard. I slowly move the item into my pocket and notice the shape of it for the first time. It is a necklace of some kind. Jewelry for someone like me is virtually nonexistent, so this is the first time I have ever touched something so smooth and sacred. Ms. Morrow must have gone to great lengths to hide this from the Royal Guard, let alone all of the nosy children who lived with us in the orphanage for so many years.

I make sure to keep my pace and follow the Royal Guard down the pebbled paths that carve the way for my future trade in the Golden Palace. The talisman will have to wait for another time to be examined. Hopefully, in the haste to get all of us organized into rooms for the night, our escorts will not think to check our pockets for stowaway items.

It did not seem as though I was in the crumbling house very long, but the darkness is now upon us, which means I took longer than thought to vacate the premises. The streets are barely lit, making it hard for me to see the Royal Guard walking quickly in front of me.

Our use of power is rationed so that the Royal Adair family has access to all they need whenever they need. The rest of us are forced to take cold showers, use candles, and stay warm by the use of fireplaces when it is cold out. The Adair's must be doing important things all the time if they can't even spare us warm showers during the winter months. I bet King Rennin is just exhausted from all of his hard work using the electricity the rest of us go without.

I squint my eyes and can see the silhouettes of other boys and girls being escorted by members of the Royal Guard towards the Golden Palace as well. As I get closer,

I realize I do not recognize many of them, but that isn't unusual considering there are four small schools in our area for the four neighborhoods surrounding the palace. We simply walk to the school assigned to our neighborhood. Some of us walk from orphanages and others walk from massive houses with their own servants. It still amazes me that there were only a handful of fights each week considering how different we all were. Then again, each of us does what we are told to survive in this hellhole.

After years of dreaming of leaving the orphanage, I never actually thought this day would come. Now that it has, I cannot help but feel a tinge of sadness. Even though I was never full and had to take care of more children than I could count, Ms. Morrow took care of me and tried to keep me out of trouble. I'll have to thank her for that one day.

Then again, I have to make certain I see her again just so I can find out what else she knows about me. Who are my parents? Why did they abandon me?

I don't know how I will arrange a meeting, but I will find a way once I am settled into my new trade. I know her habits and schedules well enough to know how often she visits the market. Perhaps I will be sent on an errand to purchase supplies and run in to her then.

Either way, I have to know more about my history. My curiosity and desire to know is already eating me alive from the inside and out.

I am briefly shoved by one of the members of the Royal Guard who is propelling ahead of me. I must be walking too slowly for his taste. I notice he is escorting a young boy to the palace as well; only, he has tied the boy to him. That's what happens when you try to resist an order from the Royal Guard you are treated like a stock animal. Another lucky soul that was spared a significant beating because of the ceremony tomorrow.

He looks so distraught, as are many of the faces I catch brief glimmers of in the dim lighting. Who can blame us? We are all leaving the only homes we have known up to this point to take our assigned places in society. What were once our homes will soon become distant pasts for us.

As I look around, I notice no one is struggling or fighting the Royal Guard as we are led like sheep through the streets. That's how conditioned we are to just go with what we are told to do. No one dares to put up a fight out of fear of being beaten and ousted.

Sometimes, I wonder if being ousted would be so bad. I know the land has nothing to offer and I would be alone, but I would be free to live on my own and wouldn't have to put the needs and desires of others before my own for the first time in my life. Many people have been ousted over the years and none of them have returned, which makes me think they are either dead or thriving without being under the finger of the Royal Adair family.

On the other hand, many have chosen to take Instant Death pills rather than risk being ousted to the Battle Grounds.

When I approach the palace, my breath catches on the fortress before me. It may be dark on the streets, but it is far from shady around this place. The main gates of the citadel are carved from gold and about as tall as the orphanage. If just the gates are this drastic, I can only fathom what the palace looks like upon closer glance.

The Golden Palace does not disappoint. It is mesmerizing in every way. The structure is massive and glimmering. Gold walls and enormous windows peer back at me. Never in my life have I seen something so illustrious. The Royal Guard begins yelling at us to line up and listen for our room assignments. This abruptly shakes me from my daze. The draw of the Golden Palace enamored me so much that I didn't even notice the crowd of other seventeen year olds so close to me.

We do as we are told and get in line. Our names are called one by one and we disperse to find our cells, or rooms as the Royal Guard refers to them, where we will sleep and rest before the choosing ceremony begins in the morning, although I do not see how any of us can rest in these rooms. At first glance, the rooms are bare, frigid, and unwelcoming. There are toilets and showers in our rooms, but it is evident privacy is not an option due to the glass wall that separates the bathroom from the two small beds lining the walls of the room. Upon closer inspection, I notice each bed has a dress on it for us to wear to the ceremony in the morning.

There are two of us assigned to this room and, luckily, I am rooming with another girl. Others weren't so fortunate. Some rooms are gender mixed or have three assigned to the rooms that are identical to mine.

After a few hours of complete silence and sitting on the beds we were assigned to, I finally attempt to strike up a conversation with my roommate. "So, you are obviously seventeen like me, which is why you are here."

When she glances up to respond, I realize this girl looks so familiar. I cannot place where I have seen her before, but as I catch a better peek of her in the light, I am certain I have met her before.

"Yes, I am seventeen and my name is Edith. Forgive me for not wanting to talk, but I am not exactly thrilled to be here. Today is my birthday and I didn't even get a chance to taste the birthday cake my mother made for me, let alone kiss my family goodbye."

I should feel some sort of compassion for her right now, but I don't. Today is my birthday as well and I didn't have a cake or a family to share it with. At least someone cared enough to try to celebrate her birthday.

"Well, Happy Birthday to you, Edith. Today happens to be my birthday too, so I understand the whole not wanting to be here aspect."

"Did you at least get to try your birthday cake?"

"I'm not even sure what one of those looks like. I grew up in an orphanage and the closest we came to celebrating birthdays was getting an extra roll at dinner. We were lucky if it was warm."

"I guess we just weren't meant to have a great seventeenth birthday today," Edith points out.

In an effort to lighten the mood, I ask Edith what sort of trade she is hoping to attain, serving the entire royal family in cleaning or the kitchen or being assigned as a companion for one of them.

Without hesitation, Edith discusses her desire to be a companion. This is where we differ. She wants to travel and witness the daily tasks of the royal family. I guess that would be fun if you were into that sort of thing. I would rather clean quietly in a room where I'll be practically invisible to all others around me.

When Edith asks me what I'd prefer, I lie and say I would be fine with anything as long as I am able to eat huge meals. I'm not sure why I lie exactly, but exposing my introvert personality doesn't seem like a good idea at the moment.

We casually talk for an hour or so, mostly so we can avoid facing the reality of our current situation. Edith shares about her family. Her last name is West, which means her parents are servants as well. Based on what she's told me thus far, she is an only child and both parents complete their trades as servants for government officials. The only reason Edith won't be a servant for a member of the government is because the Royal Adair family is in need of more servants, so whether or not members of the government need any is irrelevant this month.

When Edith begins to ask prying questions about my

life, I suddenly remember the small item I'm shielding in my pocket. In an effort to end the conversation, I yawn and tell Edith we should get some sleep to avoid having bags under our eyes in front of the royals in the morning. She agrees and folds herself into her stiff bed.

There isn't a way to hide much in this small room, so the only option I have is to change into the one set of extra clothes I brought with me and ask Edith to turn around and face her wall so I can do so. Once she turns around, I pull out the fragile piece and instantly recognize it as a locket. I have only seen pictures of lockets and never a real one. Before Edith can question what is taking so long, I put it around my neck and pull the collar of my shirt up to cover the knotted chain.

Soon, it is lights out in the facility. I use this time to hide in my rickety cot, pull the covers over my head, and study the locket. I can't see much since the entire facility has been blacked out, so I slowly run my fingers over the locket. From what I can feel, there is some sort of flower embellished on the outside of one side and initials on the other. After brushing my fingers over the initials time and time again, I identify the letters: EA. Who these initials stand for is anyone's guess. A last name that begins with the letter A is reserved for royal families. Did Ms. Morrow steal this necklace from someone? If she did, I will be ousted for certain since I am now the one who possesses it.

I wish I could see the locket to understand what is so important about it that Ms. Morrow risked her life giving it to me when she hid it in my waistband. Such an action would be seen as treacherous since it is directly ignoring the Royal Guardsman's command to only bring a change of clothes for the night.

As I continue to turn and feel the locket, I realize I cannot open the darn thing. No matter how much I try to force my nail into the crevice to open it, I cannot get it to budge. Why would someone go through all the trouble of having and hiding a locket that doesn't open?

A nearby girl crying into her makeshift bed interrupts my focus. I can't blame her - I suddenly feel lonely and dismayed also.

At some point in the night, I fall asleep clutching the locket. When I wake, the lights are on and Edith is already on her feet.

"Get any sleep, Elaine?"

"Just a little, how about you?"

"Not really. I am too nervous for this morning. What

if they take one look at me and decide I'm not good enough to be a palace servant? What if they decide to oust me and send me on my way?

"Edith, there is no reason they won't assign you your trade. Take a deep breath and calm yourself. If you go out there shaking as you are right now, they might think you are too jittery to be a companion."

"You are right. I need to step back and stop overthinking this process. Thank you, Elaine."

Before long, we are pressing the dress uniforms we were provided with and begin changing into them. As I am doing so, I forget about the locket I was previously hiding under the collar of my shirt just long enough for it to slip out and catch the light just right. I jolt and shove it back into the collar of my dress. I must not move quickly enough because Edith seems to catch a glimpse of it.

"What's that?"

Just then, our door flies open and a member of the Royal Guard walks in.

"Miss Edith, Miss Elaine, the Royal Adair family will see you now."

We are shepherded out of our night cell and escorted down a long and narrow hall. For being so gorgeous on the outside, the palace lacks some serious character in this section of the place, maybe that's just because no one important sees this area. The walls are deep gray and devoid of any decorations or pictures. Shivers run down my spine.

Walking through the palace to our destination seems to take hours, climbing windy staircases, shuffling across glossy floors, and finally arriving at the entrance doors to a room where our fates will be sealed without our consent. The only other options seem hopeless.

Edith grabs my hand and gives it a squeeze. "Good luck."

"Give them your best smile and don't make eye contact."

The jeweled doors open and we are pushed through to stand in front of the Royal Adair family. I can't breathe and it feels as though all of the air has left the room.

Chapter 3

Standing before us is the Royal Adair family. As I study them while careful not to meet their eyes, I am taken back by what an attractive family they are. There are four of them total, King Rennin, Queen Majorie, Prince David, and Princess Lily-Beth. Years ago, I remember a rumor circulating concerning another member in the family the oldest sibling. Evidently, there was one more child, but he died at a young age. Unfortunately, it is hard to recall any other details. No one talks about the Adair family in a negative light out of fear of being killed or ousted. Everything we say must be cautious and censored, similar to how we must live each day of our lives. Living in the palace though, I am certain other servants will be able to tell me more and won't hesitate to gossip. As ironic as it is, those who work closest to the royal family are known for being the least cautious and mindful of what they say. Someone is bound to know what happened to the firstborn of the Adair parents.

The family is deep in a banter of some sort. They do not notice our approach until we are just a few feet away from them. This gives me more time to study the individuals I will be serving in the coming months. I have never been this close to any of the members of the royal family before, so I take it in while I can.

King Rennin is as dark in features as he is strong. The first detail I notice about him is his dark brown hair that falls in waves across his golden crown. I have never seen such long hair on a man that is so well kept and glamorous in every way. Judging by his size as he sits on the throne, I am estimating he is over six feet tall. His well-built frame makes his lion of a throne look small. It is evident his reputation for being a fierce and ardent king is directly correlated to his scope and posture.

To King Rennin's left sits his queen, Majorie. She is easily the most beautiful woman I have ever seen. Flowing out from the gemmed crown that sits upon her brow is wildly curly, blonde hair that drapes down her back. It then cascades down the sides of her narrow face and enhances her stunning blue eyes. She has the kind of eyes that could pierce right through you and see your innermost thoughts. For some reason, I feel a chill run through me as I continue studying her. The way she grasps her husband's hand ever so tightly, I can tell she is the muscle behind many of the decisions that are made in the family. Perhaps King Rennin isn't as strong as I initially assessed.

The two next to each other embody a couple I never want to oppose because I fear I will lose before I even realize the battle has begun.

Directly on the side of Queen Majorie is Prince David the older of the two siblings. I am guessing he is around eighteen years old, but his character suggests otherwise. I do not know how I did not notice him earlier. He is easily identified as the son of King Rennin due to his impeccable resemblance to him. The only difference I am able to decipher is with his eyes. He does not possess dark brown eyes like his father or deep blue eyes like his mother; instead, his eyes are golden like the throne he stiffly perches on. As I continue to examine his posture, I notice his hands are gripping the throne arms so tight that his knuckles are a shade too white. What could the family possibly be arguing about at this moment that is making the prince so discernibly uncomfortable? If not for his telling knuckles, his eyes would perceive him to be calm and collected as his mother appears to scold him for something us lowly individuals cannot hear.

Suddenly, I have the strangest feeling as though someone is watching me. I quickly glance around the room, careful not to make direct eye contact with any of the royal family and then I see the glare is stemming from Princess Lily-Beth. I was so drawn to my interpretation of the first three members of the family that I did not notice her eyes throwing daggers at me. I am quick to put my head and eyes back down where they belong before she accuses me of disrespect. From the little I was able to deduce of her, she is just as gorgeous as her mother, yet much smaller in stature. However, she must make up for that flawed characteristic in her visibly intense nature.

Her glare is only broken when Queen Majorie addresses her, "Princess Lily-Beth, if you are truly that unhappy with your current companion, we can send her to work in the kitchen and you may choose a new one. Seeing as how you are just now requesting a new one after all of the other possible companions have already passed through, you may select one of the two before you."

"Prince David, you will just have to make due with the companion you have and select a new one during the next choosing ceremony."

For the first time during the conversation, I hear Prince David speak.

"Mother, I am not as concerned with having the most attractive companions in the area as my little sister. She is more than welcome to have her choice. Besides, I do not see an agreeable companion before me anyway."

Although it is a jab at Edith and me, I am not offended. I was called much worse during my years living at the orphanage. Edith, on the other hand, cannot help but curl her lips. She is a really pretty girl and was no doubt told that growing up, so this must be slightly painful for her pride. I give her a soft nudge to wake her back from her angry reaction.

Princess Lily-Beth does not hesitate to respond. "I knew you all would see it my way. Youngest or not, I always get what I want."

I know this statement is said in response to the other members of the royal family, but Princess Lily-Beth says it as she strives to catch my gaze, almost to challenge me to meet her eyes.

If I did hold her eye contact, I would be dismissed and ousted before I could even catch my breath, which I did not realize I was holding until just now.

She might be named after the nation's flower, but Princess Lily-Beth is far from timid and pleasant. A name like Spoiled-Brat would be more suited for this woman sitting before me. She can't possibly be any older than sixteen, and yet, here she is making demands of the king and queen. What a fierce queen she will be one day. I hope that is a day I do not live to witness.

"Alistair, which ditch did you drag these two out of?"

"Princess Lily-Beth, Alistair is a general in the Royal Guard, so you will address him as such," King Rennin scolds.

"As for the young women in front of you, my guess is neither one of them will be any better of a companion to you than your current one if you cannot treat them like human beings, servant or not."

As she rolls her eyes, Princess Lily-Beth retorts, "Right. General Richmond, who are these two lovely souls you have graced our presence with?"

I can taste her disgust with us the moment she says this.

"King Rennin and Queen Majorie, it is my pleasure to introduce you to Miss Edith and Miss Elaine."

As General Richmond says our names, we each curtsy and flash our best smiles. The wrong look or move could cause us to be instantly ousted.

We do not rise until Queen Majorie tells us we may stand and approach Princess Lily-Beth.

As we inch closer to the princess, my palms begin to sweat. My fate is in the hands of this brat and all I can do is smile and nod like a housebroken pet.

Princess Lily-Beth is quick to get to her feet and begin circling us like a preying shark. We are two small fish in very shallow waters, waiting to suffocate or be eaten at any second.

"Well, I don't feel like there is much of an option here since these two look so much alike."

For the first time since I laid eyes on Edith, I realize the princess is right. We do look quite similar in our features. Maybe that is why I feel like I have met Edith before. Maybe I haven't actually seen her before, but just subconsciously picked up on the similarities between us.

As Princess Lily-Beth continues to scrutinize, she steps closer to me. So close that my breath catches and I try not to make any sudden movements. If I happen to breathe on her, she might sense my fear and instantly devour me like the hungry predator she is.

Out of the corner of my eye, I see Edith playing with something on her wrist. Her sleeve is covering most of it, but I can just see a piece of the golden object she is fidgeting with. I suppose I am not the only one who smuggled in something so precious as jewelry.

"I'll take this one," the princess motions to me.

"Very well, Your Highness. What will you have us do with the other one?" General Richmond asks.

"I'll take her too. After all, a queen can never have too many companions."

"Not so fast, young lady!" Queen Majorie interrupts.

"You have many years to wait before you are queen, my dear. General Richmond, please escort Miss Edith to the housekeeping quarters. She will be assigned to Prince David's servant division."

This isn't what I envisioned in the slightest. Maybe they confused the two of us. Edith should be the princess' companion and I should be the one who quietly attends to the rooms and order of the palace.

"Mother, I do not need another useless woman around to clean my quarters. They all gossip and giggle enough as it is. Adding another young woman to the group would just make those old women howl even more."

"David, it would do you some good to just agree with your mother and know we do understand what is best for you. If you are to be king one day, you will need to learn how to become more agreeable."

At King Rennin's insult, Prince David grips his chair a little harder and tightens his lips.

"General Richmond, if we are done with this choosing ceremony for the day, we will be departing to our chambers."

"Yes, your majesty, these were the last two. Please excuse the time it took for me to conclude."

King Rennin does not miss a beat. "You are excused. Now, deliver these women to their appropriate quarters and go on with your daily duties that have been neglected this morning."

As the family begins to exit the room, I see Prince David actually look at the two actresses in front of him and appear as though he did not enjoy the entertainment we provided for him. Do I sense sympathy in his look or abhorrence? At this point, it could be either. The royal family put on more of a show for us than we did for them, so nothing surprises me at the moment.

"General Richmond, hurry and escort my new companion to my room. I need her to get to her trade immediately. There is already so much for her to do," Princess Lily-Beth shouts over her shoulder.

"Yes, Princess Lily-Beth. She will be there shortly."

Once the family has vacated the large room, General Richmond instructs us to wait here for just a moment while he tends to something in the next room. He is barely through the main door when Edith bursts into tears.

"I was meant to be a companion, not a maid! My parents will be so ashamed. How could they pick you over me? I deserved it so much more than you."

"Edith, I understand your frustration, but…"

"You couldn't possibly understand. You grew up in an orphanage, so you probably don't even know how to socialize or make people around you happy. I, on the other hand, have been filled with so much love and hope that I know Princess Lily-Beth would prefer me over you."

She is right. I was not raised as someone who lives to socialize and entertain others. My life has been comprised of how to provide for myself and keep myself alive, while also maintaining the health of the other kids in the orphanage. I have no idea how to keep someone like a royal happy.

I know we don't have much more time together, so I pull Edith in for a taut hug. We don't know each other very well, but something about her nature tells me she isn't trying to hurt my feelings. She is just disappointed in herself right now.

It takes a minute, but Edith embraces me as well. When she does this, I feel her bracelet brush against the back of my neck. Before she can pull away, I grab her wrist and instantaneously recognize the charm attached to the gold chain. It is a tiny key embellished with a flower on one side and initials on the other, just like my locket.

Edith is quick to pull away from my clutch and hide her bracelet within the folds of her dress. "What do you think you are doing?"

"Edith, I recognize your key. It matches perfectly with…"

"Ladies, please follow me this way," General Richmond interrupts.

When we do not respond as quickly as he would like, General Richmond stomps his foot and motions for two members of the guard to give us the slightest nudge forward. As we exit the room, Edith is turned right and I am escorted to the left, down two very different paths.

Chapter 4

When I enter my assigned room, I am overcome by emotions. The first thing I notice is I have an actual door that opens and closes. My room at the orphanage had a doorway, but no door. Ms. Morrow removed all of the interior doors so kids couldn't hide behind them and get into trouble.

Not only do I have a real door, but a decently sized bed also. Maybe I won't be too long for this bed so my feet can stay nice and warm all night long. I've never really known that feeling before being comfortable and warm. Next to my bed are a small table and dresser for me to put my belongings in. This is the first time for me to have my own table in my room. Is this what luxury is?

Glancing around the room, I see a set of double doors

and wonder where they lead. As I cross the vast room to open the doors that are suddenly calling to me, I realize there are footsteps following me. Before I can even spin around to address the person walking just a little too closely for my liking, I trip on a rug and brace for a hard impact. However, instead of falling face first into the floor, strong arms react and catch me. Only then do I comprehend where the footsteps were coming from the member of the Royal Guard who escorted me to my new room.

Holding me about a foot off of the floor is a dashingly handsome man I did not pay attention to until just now. In fact, I do not recall a time when I have ever been this close to a man before. This surprises me and I stop breathing. As I slowly begin to suffocate myself, I take note of this man's stark blue and yellow eyes. I don't believe I have ever seen eyes like his blue around the rim, with a hint of yellow just around the center. They stick out easily in contrast with his cropped blonde hair. My eyes continue down to his pointed chin that is sharp in all the right places. Only then do I grasp the gravity of my current situation. I am holding my breath as I stare at this man who is holding my limp body up. He must think I am insane.

I make every attempt to hoist myself up, only to lose

my balance from my loss of oxygen. The man endeavors to steady me.

"Are you alright, ma'am?"

"I am, thank you. Just a little overwhelmed by all of the changes today has brought."

"Princess Lily-Beth has requested your presence immediately, so please change into a new companion uniform quickly."

He crosses the room to the double doors I noticed moments ago and opens them. I do not know why I expected something extraordinary, but it appears as though the decorative doors only lead to what I am assuming is a closet. Ms. Morrow was the only one with a closet in her room at the orphanage, so this is exciting for me. The gentleman pulls out a uniform and hangs it on one of the doors for me to reach.

"Thank you, Mr...."

"Price. Officer Price."

"Thank you for your guidance and assistance, Officer Price."

"Officer Price is my official name, but you can call me Logan."

"Very well, Logan."

"You better dress quickly. Princess Lily-Beth does not like to be kept waiting."

"I am beginning to think the princess does not like anything or anyone other than herself."

I quickly realize I just spoke negatively of a member of the Adair family to a Royal Guardsman, which could hold grave consequences.

"Forgive me. I did not mean…"

"Do not worry, your assessment of the princess is correct. We will keep this between the two of us. Now, I will leave you to prepare for your first day of work. Her room is directly behind this door."

He gestures to a door cleverly placed in the center of the room. "This door connects your two rooms, but you cannot open this door unless the princess calls for you. Only the princess may open the door and access you whenever she pleases."

Privacy was unheard of at my previous home, so it is no surprise that I will not be endowed with that amenity here either. This does not bother me, though. I am too thrilled to have doors, a bed, table, and dresser to be upset about anything at the moment. My sudden burst of emotion is overpowering. I am certain I am about to pass out from all of the excitement when my bedroom door closes as Logan exits and loud yelling from the adjoining room begins.

"Tardiness on your first day as my companion is unnerving. Get in here now or you will suffer consequences you have never heard of before!"

I hastily change into my stiff uniform and scurry into the room next door. The elation of the extravagance of my room is quickly burnt out by the elegance of the princess' room. The chandelier cannot be ignored. Emeralds and jewels of all colors bedazzle it. No wonder our electricity is rationed the majority of it must be utilized to power this one piece of lighting in the princess' room. Then there's her closet. I could live in her closet and be perfectly content.

"Wipe the drool off of your dirty chin and come here."

I cross the enormous room and curtsy before Princess Lily-Beth. "Yes, my lady."

"You will refer to me as Princess Lily at all times and you are late. As my companion, you will be available day and night, whenever I call. You will not be dismissed to your quarters until I have grown tired of your presence."

"I understand, Princess Lily."

"I am not done yet. You will make yourself look presentable, which means you will take daily showers, dress your face, and style your hair. The companion you replaced will be in your room shortly to teach you how to do these things. Your bathing skills seem to be lacking."

I know it is meant as an insult, but the princess is correct. I have never had warm water when I showered, so my showers have always been quick and precise.

"As for your uniforms, the servants in the laundry room will clean and press them for you. Just make sure you know how to put your uniforms in your laundry basket each night."

Laundry basket? I'm sure I will learn what that is soon enough. In the orphanage, I just put my clothes in a pile in the corner of my small room and washed them by hand in cold water in the sink once a week.

"Your duty is to keep me entertained and do as I ask. If I need tasks to be completed or someone to fill me in on what is going on among the simple people in town, it is your job to accomplish these things. You never question me or speak to me unless spoken to first, something my last companion was unable to excel in."

"As you wish, Princess Lily."

"Good. You are dismissed. You have much to learn in your quarters. Do not take your training lightly. If you cannot make yourself more appealing, you will be ousted before you can make yourself comfortable in your locker of a room."

The look of complete repulsion she gives me as I curtsy before I leave her room is enough to strike instant fear in me. I cannot help but feel like she is looking for a reason to oust me. All I can do is complete the duties required of me and hope the princess does not have a bad day. I smile and leave through the same door I entered through just a couple of minutes ago. The door will not close quickly enough. It was a quick encounter, but enough to rattle me.

As I lean against the door and begin to allow my panic to set in, a woman slightly older than me makes her presence known.

"There is no time to relax. Stand up straight and do not take what I say lightly. My name is Judith and you are taking my place as Princess Lily-Beth's companion. If you make one mistake or breathe too loudly for her, she will discard you as she has done to me. My problem was I grew too comfortable with her and spoke to the princess before she addressed me. She plays games with us and wins them every time."

Well, I suppose that means a nap is out of the question.

"Now that the heavy part is out of the way, let's talk bathing." Judith grabs my shoulders and turns me around to face a bathroom I had not noticed was tucked in on the opposite side of my room. It is not big, but the first bathroom I have ever had all to myself.

Judith shows me the different knobs on the bathtub, which are also made out of gold, and motions to the hot water.

"That one will help to calm you after a long day with the princess. I'm assuming hot water is just a fable to you, just as it was to me when I began my trade here."

She then points to different buttons on the side of the bathtub. "Those release different fragrant oils into the bathtub. Do not use the purple button. Princess Lily-Beth hates lavender. She thinks her nature is calming enough and does not like for those around her to smell better than her. The orange button is clementine and the yellow is lemon. Both of those are acceptable for use."

"What do I wash my hair with?" Then, I look up and see the different colored tubes draping from the showerhead. Judith begins to reach and explain.

"Each of those represents different steps in the bathing process. You must first shampoo, then condition, and lastly, apply the conditioner that stays in your hair. Do not wash the last one out because Princess Lily-Beth will notice if you do and she will not tolerate a companion who cannot demonstrate flawless hygienic practices."

I'm not even sure what conditioner is, but it sounds wonderful.

"Now, get undressed and take your bath. Your laundry basket is against the far wall. Once you are done bathing, put on one of the robes that is hanging on the back of the door and let me know you are done so I can show you the next steps of the process to make you physically agreeable to the princess."

I do as I am told and begin to prepare the bathtub. Because I have never bathed in hot water before, it takes a bit of playing to decipher what the best temperature for the bath will be. When I finally settle in to the bathtub, I almost begin to cry. Is this what being warm when you bathe feels like? I can't remember the last time I was this warm and cozy. After much trial and error, I finally figure out how to make myself smell like lemon and wash my hair thoroughly. I almost forget to apply the conditioner that I cannot wash out at the very end. When I turn the handle on the end of the last draping tube, too much conditioner comes out and sprays out of control. I hasten to turn it off and clean up the mess. Finally, I feel like I am suitable enough for Judith to come back in.

"Judith, I am ready for you to make me pretty!"

Judith enters and shoots me a look of disbelief. "You are suffocating me with the lemon radiating off of you. Use less next time. Now, to dry your hair, you sit here and place this cap on your head."

I follow her lead and sit on the awkward chair with the cap attached to it. Judith places her foot on the pedal and the cap roars to life. I am startled when the cap begins to blow my hair every direction. Is this thing going to pull my hair out? Why won't it stop?

According to Judith, the drying process takes thirty seconds and is well worth the wait, although I'm not sure what wait she is referring to.

When Judith removes her foot from the pedal, she turns my chair around to face a well-lit mirror. I am surprised by how long it takes me to recognize myself. Must be because all of the filth has been washed off and my hair is sleek and clean. Judith brushes one side of my hair and then instructs me to brush the other side. Who knew that it was possible for me to brush my own hair wrong for seventeen years?

Once the brushing is complete, Judith shows me a few different options for hair styling. I can apply a tight bun, braid, or pinup, as long as my hair is out of my face. After years of just pulling my hair straight back, braiding it seems uncomfortable. I opt for the tight bun since it is similar to my usual style, but Judith decides to teach me how to braid anyway.

After an hour or so of learning about the different braiding styles, Judith is kind enough to graduate me to the next level of training makeup. This process seems all wrong to me. Why would a woman apply paint on her face to make her look like something she is not, something unnatural? Luckily, Princess Lily-Beth does not like to be out shown, so only light foundation, blush, mascara, lipstick, and powder is required.

It's been two hours and I am still struggling. My makeup is too dark, too light, too bland, too much, or too everything every time I attempt to finish the application. Judith is beginning to lose her patience with me and scolds me for not doing exactly as she instructed.

"You are not stupid if you have made it this far to become a companion for the Royal Adair family, so I know you can do this. Pay attention and stop screwing it up!"

I attempt to apply the makeup once again, but this time, I use slower motions and watch my face instead of Judith's. When done, Judith finally approves.

Now, I can bathe, style my hair, and apply makeup. Next step is to conquer the nation - who knew?

It is evident Judith is growing weary of me and the day has come and gone. All that is left is for Judith to present me to Princess Lily-Beth and ensure she is satisfied with my appearance. Judith knocks on the adjoining door and is instantly told to enter.

When we walk into the room, I notice Logan standing next to Princess Lily-Beth's study table, quite close to her, in fact. My face begins to blush, which Princess Lily-Beth uses to her advantage.

"So now that you know how to bathe properly, you think you can look at a member of the Royal Guard and turn pink? You should be blushing because you're embarrassed, not because you're proud of yourself."

I might be imagining it, but Logan appears to shift uncomfortably.

"Excuse me, Princess Lily-Beth. I must return to my post." Logan exits the room quicker than I anticipated and Princess Lily-Beth directs her full attention towards me. She crosses the room and circles me. She must get satisfaction out of circling and preying on people like me, but it doesn't bother me this time. If it is a game she wants to play, it is a game I will happily join.

"Not your best work, Judith, but I will accept it."

"Thank you, Princess Lily-Beth."

"You are dismissed. Oh, and Judith, try not to be jealous of Elaine. Your time with me just ran out," the princess spits out.

"Yes, Princess Lily-Beth."

As Judith leaves the room, I attempt to thank her for her help with my eyes, but I am interrupted by the princess moving closer to me. I wonder why Judith refers to the princess by her full name and not "Princess Lily" like I was told to utilize. Maybe that is another one of her games convince me to disrespect her so she can oust me. I'm not sure what quality I possess that the princess does not like, but I am smarter than she gives me credit for. I will not stumble and cave in to her pressure.

"Very well, go to bed. I am tired of looking at you for today. Go to sleep now and be ready at first light."

I curtsy and begin to leave her room. As I am walking back toward my room, the princess warns, "Don't be stupid enough to try to leave your quarters. Officer Price is stationed right outside of my door to protect me, but mostly to babysit you."

I gently close the door behind me and take in the first moment of privacy I've had in what feels like a very long time.

Suddenly, the room feels too small and I am once again struggling to breathe. I wish this feeling were new to me. I worked for hours to make myself presentable for the princess. Now, I have to bathe again to remove all of the makeup and chemicals in my hair that took hours to get right. This must be a game. I refuse to let the princess win this match, so I peel myself off of the door and head for the bathroom. There are so many doors in this room that I easily confuse myself and open the wrong door.

Standing in front of me is Logan. "I hope you aren't trying to sneak out, Miss Elaine."

"No, I got turned around and opened the wrong door. I was looking for the bathroom. Sorry for the confusion." I'm not sure why I am so blunt and I am embarrassed that he now knows I have no sense of direction and need to find a bathroom.

"It is no problem, Miss Elaine. I was going to knock

on your door to let you know your dinner has arrived before you opened it."

"Dinner?"

"Yes, they do feed us here."

"Oh, I would hope so. I just didn't think about eating today with all of the chaos and just realized this is my first meal of the day."

Then, a woman around forty years old walks between us and sets a tray holding a sandwich, cup of tea, and a side salad on the table next to my bed.

"When you are done with it, leave the tray in the hall so I may collect it. There aren't seconds, so don't ask for any."

The lady walks off quickly and cuts me off when I try to thank her. I hear her mumble something about being spoiled under her breath as she plods off. If only she knew where I came from.

My attention returns to Logan, who seems to be around twenty years old, yet wise beyond his years, judging by the rings around his eyes. I can imagine he has seen more in this line of duty than most have in an entire lifetime.

"Have you eaten? Would you like to come in and share the food she just dropped off?"

"No, ma'am. It would be inappropriate for me to do so and I do not believe the princess would approve."

"Oh, you probably already ate with the princess in her quarters."

"No, I didn't say that. I just keep a respectful distance from the princess and her companions at all times."

"It didn't look like respectful distance between you and the princess when you were in her chamber earlier." I don't mean for it to sound jealous, but it definitely comes off that way. I have known this man one day and already feel like awkwardness is building between us. I am really just trying to read the relationship between the two. Are they friends? Acquaintances? Just a professional relationship? For some reason, I was instantly drawn to him when he caught me earlier and cannot shake the feeling of trust between us, which is why I am trying to read all I can about him.

Logan looks bothered by my previous comment. "Princess Lily-Beth asked for my opinion on something she wrote, so I was reading when you walked into the room."

I feel like a complete idiot. He doesn't have to explain himself to me. I need to step back and recover somehow.

"I didn't mean it like that. I just meant that I wasn't expecting to see you in the princess' bedroom. I should eat my dinner and get ready for bed. Goodnight, Logan."

"Goodnight, Miss Elaine."

"Just call me Elly. That's what my friends call me." I'm not really sure what friends I'm referring to, but it just slips out and feels like the right thing to say in the moment.

"Very well then. Goodnight, Elly."

I gently close the door and I am almost certain I hear Logan wish me a happy birthday. How he knew, I do not know, but this knowledge somehow makes me somewhat excited.

With all of the jubilation of the day still buzzing through my mind, I cannot think of a better way to relax than in the soothing bathtub for the second time this evening.

After spending way too much time in the warm water, I rummage through the drawers and find some pajamas to sleep in. They are the nicest pajamas I have ever worn before. Beautiful green, silky, and soft – not like anything I have ever felt before. If this is what I sleep in as a servant, I cannot even begin to imagine what the royal family sleeps in.

Carefully, I place my locket in the drawer of the table next to me and set my alarm for first light. I drift off into a deep sleep before I even realize my eyes are closing.

Chapter 5

The princess gave me specific instructions to be ready for my trade when the sun rose, so now I patiently wait for her to summon me to her quarters. I am not certain what today will bring, but I do know that I must be on my best game if I want to survive by the side of Princess Lily-Beth. I woke up hours before the first light peaked through my window to bathe, dry and style my hair, and paint my face.

I press my ear ever so gently against the adjoining door, careful not to dishevel the braid that took me what felt like days to finish. I patiently listen for movement that suggests the princess is awake. Instead, I hear heavy breathing that implies the princess is still in a deep sleep. I use the extra time to my advantage and begin inspecting my room further.

I wonder if Edith has a room like mine. In fact, I hope she has the luxury of hot water and a private bathroom to use. These are amenities servant families like ours were never allotted, so I can only pray she has experienced these wondrous gifts like I have in the recent hours. I notice I am holding my locket that is hidden beneath my crisp uniform that only Edith, myself, and Ms. Morrow know about. For a reason I cannot identify, this is a comforting thought.

Suddenly, something catches my attention in the corner of my eye – a small bookshelf in the crook of the room. I step closer to examine the treasure someone was kind enough to leave behind. There are three books remaining on the shelf, each serving a different purpose, judging by the various descriptions provided on the covers of the books.

The first book, leather-bound and decorated with golden ribbons and flowers, tells the tale of how our great Aparthia Nation fought and conquered our neighboring nations during the battles.

The second book, just as appealing in elegance and décor as the first, details the importance of maintaining structure and ranks within our society. I suppose this one is here to remind the dwelling companions and slaves to stay in our places and mind our rankings so we do not disrupt the peace and success of our nation.

Lastly, not as vital for someone to read as the first two, based on the bland cover that lacks a title and description, the final book seems more personal. When I open the book, I am drawn to the pages because they are handwritten, unlike the previous books grasped. Before I can decipher the writing, I hear the princess finally summoning me to her room. I quietly place the books back on the shelf and expedite my pace to the room next door, then hesitate when I remember the locket concealed by my new uniform. Before I can decide whether or not I should hide it in my room, the princess begins to tap her foot to demonstrate her dissatisfaction with me.

When I enter her room, the princess is positioned at a small table in the center of the room and is scolding the woman who brought me my dinner last night. Evidently, the woman did not have pep in her step when she served the princess.

"Do not bother coming into my room again unless your attitude changes and you know exactly who you are serving."

"Yes, Princess Lily-Beth. I will not forget again. Please forgive me for my disrespect. I did not rest much and…"

The princess waves her off before she can finish her excuse.

I do not realize her attention has been turned to me until she huffs in an exasperated manner to let me know she is annoyed with me at the moment. I quickly curtsy and put on my best smile.

"Good Morning, Princess Lily. How did you sleep?"

"Never mind small talk. First thing we need to discuss is our schedule for today. Make yourself useful and grab the papers from beside my bed."

I do as I am told and retrieve the papers.

"Assuming you know how to read, tell me what is in store for us today."

It takes me a minute to process what I am reading due to the elegance of the paper. I have never seen anything written so beautifully and on such fine paper. How is it even possible for paper to feel so…rich?

"If you do not know how to read, tell me now so I can have your friend from yesterday replace you."

"Oh, I am sorry, ma'am. I do know how to read. I was just temporarily overwhelmed by how much you must do each day. You must exhaust yourself." The lies come to me easier than I thought they would.

"Get on with it then. You are wasting my precious time."

"This morning, you are to meet with the king and queen to discuss the plans for your future. Then, you are to attend the briefing with members of the Royal Guard, followed by lunch with your brother." The thought of facing Prince David again makes my voice catch. I clear my throat and continue reading.

"In the afternoon, you have a dress fitting for the Royal Gala next week and lessons with your tutor immediately following. Just before dinner, you have a training session booked. Looks like your evening after dinner is clear of scheduled events."

"If that is all, you must fetch me my robe and call in my personal styling team."

I briefly look around the room for a robe and find a cashmere red gown hanging in the massive closet before me. I have to take seven steps into the closet before I reach the rack it is hanging on. This must be her robe. Hesitantly, I clutch the item that is nicer than any dress I have ever owned and slowly hold it out for the princess to put on.

"The point of having a companion is so I do not have to do anything myself. Put it on me."

I carefully place the article on the princess and attempt to fasten the draping cords around the princess.

"I know how to tie my own robe!"

Who knew? I just assumed I was to tie it on her as well since I had to pull it on her arms. Maybe she doesn't know how to put her own clothes on. Anyone can tie a simple bow.

I swiftly cross the room and head for the door.

"Where do you think you are going, companion?"

"Princess Lily, I was going to fetch your styling team for you."

"You dumb girl – just push the green button on the wall and my styling team will know I am ready for them."

Only then do I register that there are four buttons on the wall right next to the door that leads in and out of the room.

"I expected Judith to teach you all essential information. Just another one of her shortcomings I suppose. The green button is for dressing, the blue for the kitchen, the white for housekeeping, and the red for emergency purposes only. You press and they come. Easy as that."

I may be new to the way things work in this palace, but their priorities seem a bit distorted. Buttons for wants, not needs, with the exception of the red emergency button.

I press the green button firmly, and within minutes, a team of no less than six individuals enters the room, every one of them inspecting me and curling their lips as they do so. I thought my braid and makeup looked lovely. It's not like I get to choose my uniform. I find a corner out of the way and stand where I can be summoned if needed.

The team gets to work and forgets my presence as they work tirelessly on making the princess look stunning. Too bad they can't work their magic on her interior as well.

"Companion, fetch me the pink summer dress from the closet at once," the only man in the group spits at me.

I return to the closet and panic when I see two pink dresses. One dress is long and the other is short. Both possess thin straps and are fitted, so they can both be worn in the summer. Since Lily is going to meet with her parents, I assume something longer would be more appropriate. The palace is also a bit chilly so it might keep her warmer than the shorter of the two. I attempt to hand the selected dress to the man when he sneers at me.

"New girl, you better catch on quickly. When I tell

you to get me a summer dress, you bring me a light and short dress, not a ball gown."

I am watchful not to show my cheeks flush and return the longer dress and replace it with the shorter of the two. As I am walking back, I hear the man whispering to the princess.

"They don't make them too bright out there, do they?"

"Would you expect anything else from people who don't even know how to bathe with hot water?"

It's not like we have a choice in that department. I want to throw the dress at the pair and drag them both into a cold shower, but I continue to smile and offer up the dress.

"Elaine, you are to do whatever Jackson asks you to. His job is to enhance my already flawless looks and you are here to help, not get in the way."

"Yes, Princess Lily." I return to my corner and pray Jackson does not call for my assistance again. He has five other people around him to help, so it is obvious he just wanted to test me. I relax for the time being and observe the circus before me. While Jackson works on the princess' makeup, the others tend to their duties. Three of the women work on her hair, nails, and toes while another presses her dress. The last stylist is rubbing Princess Lily's back   and sharing the latest gossip of the palace staff. How is that even a trade?

According to the gossiping woman, Jenna, there is a new girl working in Prince David's hall who had to learn her place very quickly this morning. Apparently, the young woman was so bold as to enter Prince David's room while he was still in there. She claimed she was just trying to retrieve his bed sheets, but everyone else believes she was just trying to sneak a peek at the prince. This did not go over well with the prince. He had the girl dragged out of his room by her hair.

I am bursting at the seams. Could the girl Jenna is talking about be Edith? She couldn't be that naïve, could she? The princess is also jumping out of her skin to know more details.

"What did the girl see? Was David appropriate? What's that silly girl's name?"

"Luckily for the girl, he was already dressed and having breakfast. His companion is the one who dragged her out. Her name is something like Elsie, Edna, Emmy - "

"Edith, her name is Edith," I sputter out before I comprehend that I just spoke out of turn without being spoken to. The group grows silent and they all begin to smirk as they await the princess' wrath they are certain will follow. Princess Lily-Beth narrows her eyes at me.

"I should have known the mistake would be your friend. You two must have a lot in common, both utterly stupid, ignorant, and on the verge of being ousted."

I swallow my pride and nod my head in her direction, avoiding eye contact at all costs.

After minutes of silence, the team is dismissed and the princess is ready for her meeting with the king and queen. Everyone departs from the room with the exception of Jackson, the princess, and myself. Jackson eyes the princess one last time and seems impressed with himself. The princess heads to the bathroom one last time, leaving the miracle worker to feast on me with no one around to witness.

"Elaine, right? I am sorry to be so uncouth towards you. The princess expects us to treat her companions as she does – like rubbish. If we do not do as she says, she will have us ousted or perform death by pill. It is a cruel world and we just do what we need to as a way to stay out of trouble."

This completely thwarts me. Seconds ago, I thought this man was scum, but now, I have to reevaluate my opinion of him. Definitely not someone I can trust. "I understand, Mr. Jackson. I was not offended."

"I could tell you were, and for that, I apologize. Just some advice – keep your nose down and trust no one in this place. Everyone only thinks of themselves and how to rise up in ranks around here."

"I can see that. Thank you."

Jackson dances around on his heels and struts out of the room.

Princess Lily walks out of the bathroom and straight out. I have to jog just to catch up to her. If she had noticed, I'm sure she would have scolded me for not acting like a proper lady. As we approach the main hall, I scour the area for Logan, only to end up disappointed when another guard is present in his place. I'm still not sure why I am drawn to Logan, but I push the thought of him back and carry on to keep pace with the princess.

We travel down long hallways and through various different rooms, each with a different theme enveloping it. However, no matter the theme, there is a continuous gold coloration to each room to match the appropriate name of the bastion. I am mesmerized with each step I take. So much time and detail went into decorating this place. It is a wonder the royal family members don't spend days at a time in the diverse rooms just taking in their intricate features.

When we finally arrive in the room where the king and queen wait for us, I am somehow belted by the magnanimous ornamentation of this room. It is fit, by far, for a king and queen. This must be their private study. The walls are laced with golden fabric, intertwined with flowers and leaves of all kinds. Perched on the fabric are paintings of sorts. I do not recognize most of the individuals in the paintings, but I do recognize the royal family on their assigned wall, with the exception of one. The painting is of a young boy with blue eyes that seem faintly familiar, along with his dark blonde hair. This must be the first child of the king and queen – the one who no one speaks of. The fact that there is a painting of him in this room raises so many questions. What happened to him? Why doesn't anyone talk about him? Where is he now?

Chapter 6

"Well, Lily, how nice of you to join us. You are only twenty minutes late today. That's progress," King Rennin comments.

"I would have been on time, but my new companion does not know the difference between summer dresses and ball gowns. The gene pool in the most recent recruits must not be very good."

I slipped momentarily, but not long enough to make the princess late, not that anyone cares.

"Lily, can't you play nice with anyone we assign to be your companion?" Queen Majorie questions.

"It is easy to be nice when I don't have to teach them the basics of life."

"If it is alright with you two, I'd like to discuss more pressing business," King Rennin interrupts.

"The first order of business involves finding you a suitable man who is fit to be by your side while you help to rule our nation one day."

That seals it for me. King Rennin is a man without a heart. He is willing to sacrifice someone to be with his terrible daughter. What man has done so much wrong to be punished like this? I shudder at the thought.

"Father, we have been over this. I don't need a man to hold me back. I am stronger on my own and refuse to let a man make decisions on my behalf."

"No one is saying you will be suppressed by any means, if that is even possible, but we need to maintain relations with our neighboring nations," King Rennin responds.

"That is what David is for. Use him as your pawn. I'm sure he would enjoy that."

"As first in line to the throne, it is customary for the prince to have his choice of someone in our nation to maintain hope and tranquility among our citizens. Obviously, we prefer for it to be someone from the B class, but an F selection isn't out of the question. We make sacrifices to ensure the wellbeing of our nation, something you should consider, Lily," the queen pointedly comments.

Sacrifices? What sacrifices have these people ever made? Do they even understand that concept? They must have too much electricity pulsing through them or hot water running out of their ears to be in touch with reality.

"David secures the happiness of our nation and you sustain relations with the other two nations. This has been the plan established by your father since he first took the throne."

The princess suddenly beckons me and I stumble out of pure surprise.

"Elaine, what do you think of this plan that supposedly smoothens things over with all parties involved? Is this even a realistic plan?"

I am terrified of offending any or all members of the royal family, so I tread lightly. "Although this is the first I have heard of such arrangements, I can see how they would be prosperous. For you to marry someone from another nation, that would give them reason to remain loyal and keep communication open across the lines. If Prince David was to marry someone from within our own nation, that would add excitement for all the women of age, of a sort."

For the first time, the queen speaks directly to me.

"What are you implying with your vagueness?"

"Well, if guidelines such as specific class parameters are established, that limits the amount of hope that could potentially thrive across all classes. Why not make everyone believe they have a chance to marry the prince even if they truly don't?"

King Rennin is calculated in his response. "That is a clever point. Let all of the women of age believe they have a chance to become a member of our class, but set quiet guidelines for the prince. I do believe you finally have an intelligent companion, Lily."

"Yes, let's just lie to the people and make everyone happy. That makes perfect sense," the prince admonishes as he approaches the table.

How long has he been standing behind me? I didn't even realize he entered the room. I hope I didn't say too much or overstep any boundaries.

Prince David takes a seat next to his mother and looks at me as though I am a bug to be stepped on. "Mother. Father. Lily."

"David, you have impeccable timing, as usual."

"Thank you, Mother. I pride myself on sensing when people are planning out my life without my consent."

"Son, we were only strategizing a way to meet the needs of the people, while also finding you an appropriate spouse. One day, you and your chosen partner will be king and queen of our great nation, so we have to ensure we take the best path to get there."

"I might not be as wise as you, Father, but I do not see how providing the women of our nation with false hope is a step in the right direction."

King Rennin looks surprised by the prince's neglect to follow suit. This doesn't faze Prince David in the slightest. His jaw is set and it is evident he has plans of his own.

"Very well. What do you suggest then? A competition?"

"Definitely not a competition seeing as how I am not a prize to be won by grappling women. Instead, I suggest you allow me the opportunity to meet the available and age-appropriate women in all classes and provide me with room to choose my own future queen. If I am to continue leading with the strength you and mother have, I need an equally strong partner by my side."

The king and queen are silent, obviously digesting what the prince just said. Surprisingly, the princess has been so quiet that I almost forgot she was still seated at the table, until she speaks up.

"If David has the freedom to choose, I want the same liberty. No guidelines."

"What do you make of all of this, my queen?" King Rennin asks.

"I believe we have raised two equally stubborn offspring. Although, I do feel both have presented valid points. If we allow one of them to have open range, the other should be allotted the same luxury."

"Appealing as that sounds, we do not live in a perfect nation. The truth is Aparthia is more fragile than I care to admit, so we need to tread lightly with decisions such as these. We need to think of the happiness of our children, but also the wellbeing of our nation and relations with our neighbors as well. That being said, Lily will have free reign to select the man she chooses from either Anniah or Allenthia."

"Lily, because you are still young, you will spend the next few months traveling between our three nations. You will get to know the citizens of our partnering nations and build relations with them during that time. At the completion of that timeframe, you will then begin a selection process out of the available men. You will marry the man you choose when you turn eighteen, just like your brother will be doing in the coming months. Your first trip will be two weeks from now so that you have time to prepare and plan. You will be assigned a unit from our Royal Guard to guide and protect you during your transition from nation to nation."

Princess Lily is speechless. Her facial expressions are blank and unreadable. I cannot fathom what is going through her head at the moment. On one hand, this declaration means I will finally get to travel and see more than just the streets of our city. On the other, this endeavor will take me away from my desire to corner Ms. Morrow and find out what she knows about my parents. This also means I will not be able to cross paths with Edith anytime soon. It feels like there is so much information about my past at my fingertips, and yet, it is slipping away before my eyes.

"I will do as you say, Father, but only on one condition. If at the completion of my travels and selection process I do not find a suitable partner, I'd like to remain in one of the neighboring nations and rule alone."

King Rennin's face turns bright red at the thought of Lily ruling alone. "I do not believe you are fully processing the purpose of this opportunity, Daughter."

"I understand completely. You want me to marry

someone from one of the other two nations to keep friendly ties with them while you also maintain control over them. I will build trust and relationships with the citizens in both nations in the coming months and will attempt to find someone worthy of my presence. If I do not choose someone, I will still have that foundation that I built during my travels and the trust of the people. If I remain in one of the nations, married or not, our family will still sustain our power over them. Did I miss something?"

Princess Lily-Beth is smarter than I initially gave her credit for. She is agreeing to achieve what the king and queen envisioned for her, yet she is still compromising on her own behalf. I envy her audacious courage.

"Don't you think that sounds fair, Elaine?"

Once again, I am foiled by the princess' ability to bring me into such a touchy conversation, let alone to acknowledge me at all. Before I respond, I look to the royal parents to ensure I am allowed to speak. They stare at me and wait for a response, so I proceed.

"Princess Lily-Beth, in the way you presented it, yes, I do believe the people of Anniah and Allenthia would be happy to get to know you. I am certain they would enjoy the opportunity to share their pronounced nations with you, but I do feel as though they would be slightly disappointed if a suitor from their lands was not selected in the end. Perhaps a fair and true effort that the people can witness for themselves would ease that disappointment."

Oh no. I just indirectly stated that the princess would purposefully neglect to choose a gentleman to marry. I was speaking so fast that my words were pouring out before I could process them. I wait for my scolding or punishment, but the table remains silent for a very long period of time. Finally, Prince David interjects.

"I think your companion has a very valid point, little sister."

I might be overthinking it, but I sense anger towards me steaming from the princess' pores.

"She is just a companion and not a very bright one as you can see. She lacks the ability to think before she speaks."

Certainly not imagining the anger. I wasn't trying to upset her, but I was trying to present an honest opinion since the classes the princess will interact with are similar to the one I come from.

King Rennin's facial expression is softening and he has apparently made up his mind. "I have decided you will proceed with the travels for the next three months and then will go through a selection process. If you give that progression a true effort and do not identify a man you could possibly spend the rest of your life with, then you may stay in the nation of your choice as the representing princess of that nation."

Judging by the grin on her face, the princess is doing all she can to avoid jumping out of her seat and verbally claiming a victory. That is until the king decides to provide one more limitation.

"In your case, you are only allowed to select an individual from the upper classes. No daughter of mine will rule a territory with a man who cannot handle the willful woman you are. You will need someone with a backbone and knowledge of how our society runs. I doubt any of the lower classes would understand the gravity of such. This is a detail we will not release to the public until the selection process begins so that we may avoid any resistance to you once your visits begin."

I know I shouldn't feel offended at the king's comment, but I do. If he would spend time with people in the lower classes, he would understand that we know more than he gives us credit for. In fact, many of us are more intelligent and hardworking than his personal government members, in large part due to our need to sacrifice and thrive on the little we are allotted.

As I glance at the queen, I notice she looks somewhat melancholy. I am not sure why she would be sad at the thought of her bratty daughter leaving the palace for a little while, until I understand what really brought on this sadness. The queen is gazing at the painting of the young boy on the wall. She must miss him. He might have already been through the selection process and married by now. That is pain no mother should ever have to feel. I pity her for what she has undergone, but also for what she is feeling right now. The princess quickly interrupts that short-lived feeling.

"Now that my future has been outlined for me, it's David's turn."

"Ah, yes, you are correct. David, let's discuss your standards. Your position is more pressing anyway since you must wed in just a few short months. The clock began ticking for you when you turned eighteen last month. The only reason you have made it this far without us pressuring you to find a wife is because you have been doing such a fine job leading the Royal Guard. Now that the Legion has temporarily settled down, in large part due to your diligence, you have time on your hands to begin your search for a wife."

Legion? What or who is that? Settled down because of the Royal Guard? That must mean there are people who oppose the king and queen. How has this gone on without the knowledge of the people? I am beginning to understand way more happens behind these doors than I initially thought.

"I want time to find my own bride and do not want you two dabbling in any way."

Queen Majorie looks slighted. "Sweetheart, we do not dabble. We only insert ourselves when really necessary. This situation is one of those times when we have every right to guide you in the direction we see as best fit for you and our nation. We also know a thing or two about finding love in a limited amount of time, so we can use that experience to all of our advantages."

"I do not need you hosting any kinds of pageants or competitions. I would like to be able to meet women on my own and make my decision solely based on my own assessment."

"Unfortunately, that is not an option. Women will see

the crown and only the crown, not who wears it."

King Rennin has a point, as much as I don't want to admit it. It would be hard for any woman to see beyond the crown, especially after the deprived lives many of us have lived. It would be silly for any woman to pass up the prospect for something better and more powerful.

"Here is what I propose then. You two may have your staff members comb through all of the records they have on the citizens. Then, they will isolate only the single and age-appropriate women that meet certain expectations. That group can then be invited to the palace for an extended amount of time so that I may meet and engage with all of them. I do not want class to be an issue. All classes must be involved."

And I'm holding my breath again... Why would the prince want to include all classes when he took one look at Edith and me at our choosing ceremony, snarled at us, and decided we were not good enough to serve him? He must have a hidden agenda. For as handsome as he is, he is also extremely cunning, a characteristic I am starting to see rear out of him.

King Rennin does not like what he is hearing, but the princess seems absolutely entertained.

"What expectations can we set then if you are rejecting the biggest one we would like to enforce?"

"She must be seventeen to nineteen years old, not have any documented incidents with the Royal Guard, and not be taller than I am."

The last one will be easy. The prince is easily over six feet tall and many of us were so malnourished growing up that we never grew beyond five feet and seven inches tall.

Now it's the queen's turn to reveal her dissatisfaction with the direction of the conversation. "You must provide more specific standards than those if you hope to narrow the scope of women you will have to meet."

"Good point. She must also have been ranked in the top three of her class while she was in school. That will ensure that she has some level of intelligence and stamina as well. With four schools in the area, three girls at each school, and a three-year span in age, that should narrow it down to no more than thirty-six young women I may choose between. If any of those women have had run-ins with the Royal Guard documented in their files or are taller than me, they will not be invited to participate. Obviously, the married ones are out too."

"What do you think, honey? Does this sound

plausible?"

The king hesitates before he holds out his hand towards the prince. "It is settled. We will have the staff begin combing through our citizen files."

And just like that, the fates of the prince and princess have been decided upon. Such heavy decisions were made in a gold room, while sitting around a round table. No one to hear the discussion other than a few Royal Guard members posted around the room, the royal family, and me. I wonder if this is how many of their decisions are made.

Small talk continues for another few minutes and then the king and queen dismiss their children to continue on with their daily activities.

As we begin to leave from the room, I see Prince David looking at me out of the side of my eye. I have grown accustomed to being looked at with disgust by all who have recently studied me like this, so I turn to face him in a manner that tells him I am not afraid of you, but I am careful not to come off as too brazen so I do not get ousted on my first full day in my trade. I am shocked because that look of distaste I was expecting to see has been replaced by something different. Actually, he seems to be looking at me with intrigue. Maybe I am making this up in my head.

"Don't flatter yourself, Elaine. My brother just took one look at you and realized what he got himself into. He might have to spend the rest of his life married to someone like you. What a tragedy that would be!"

My blushing gave me away again. She is right. The prince just had a rude awakening when he understood the gravity of what he just agreed to. After all, I do meet all of the criteria that the royal family just established. I am no taller than five feet and two inches, haven't had any marks on my documents, luckily, involving my several incidents with the Royal Guard, am freshly seventeen, and was the first in my class at school. What an awkward situation that would be for all parties involved. The prince would have to put up with me during one of the stages of the selection process. Honestly, I'm not sure if I'm absolutely terrified or marginally excited. Either way, the coming months will be chaotic with the traveling beginning soon, along with all of the gossip that will soon develop because of these decisions that were just made.

Chapter 7

My head is still buzzing from the exhilaration of what is to come in the next few weeks so I do not fully realize we have arrived at our next scheduled event of the day - a briefing with the Royal Guard.

This room is devoid of any kind of decorations or gold. Instead, this room is rather intimidating. The lighting leaves much to the imagination because it is so dark in here. There is one very long table with chairs positioned all around it. Screens of various locations around the palace and in the city are projected on the far wall. I always had the feeling I was being watched growing up, but did not foresee it like this. When further examining the room, I now see that the chairs around the table actually have people standing directly behind them. I don't know how I missed them the first time. They are all practically blinding me with their flashy uniforms, all identical with one exception. There are four soldiers with various colors of ribbons draped over their shoulders. Four decorated soldiers, each with a different color - interesting.

"You may be seated," I hear echoed from the opposite side of the room. Prince David has entered and is taking the lead on this briefing, I see. He takes the seat at the head of the table and Princess Lily sits to his right. She motions at me to stand against the wall, so I do as I am directed and attempt to make myself blend in with my surroundings. I must not be succeeding because Logan positions himself right next to me, so close that I can feel the warmth his massive structure is radiating. I didn't feel the cold of the room until this very moment.

"Where are we with the Legion? Have any members been identified or attained?"

"Prince David, we have soldiers embedded within the citizens all over town, but have not been able to gain any significant leads at this time," Commander Richmond replies.

Mentions of the Legion again. I am still in awe that someone has been rallying against the Adair family and not many seem to know about it. Should I be worried?

"What good is the Royal Guard if you all do not know who is threatening the stability of our nation?" Princess Lily apparently wanted to make her presence known as well. Not surprising. She seems to enjoy being noticed and in control.

"Lily, do not question our hard work. These things take time and patience," Prince David scolds.

Commander Richmond seems unfazed by the interruption as he continues. "Based on what our ground soldiers are telling us, the Legion is licking their wounds in hiding. Sir, the last battle you led was precise and successful. We do not expect to hear from them again anytime soon."

Prince David does not look satisfied with that response. I have quickly learned that his tell sign of dissatisfaction is setting is chiseled jaw and narrowing his salient eyes, a quality I am coming to find attractive.

"But we do not know where they are or when they might attack again? We must work harder to find and diminish all sparks of potential uprisings again. Commander Richmond, plant three more undercover Royal Guardsmen in each neighborhood in our area. Someone from the Legion is bound to slip, and when he does, we will be there to catch him."

Commander Richmond motions to the four soldiers with the different colored ribbons to carry out and oversee this order by the end of the day. Now it makes sense. The different colors represent the four neighborhoods they oversee - one in each area. How have I never noticed them in my neighborhood before? They must not be the type of leaders who are hands-on or lead by example.

"I do understand that we should look at this situation as a win since the Legion has disappeared, but I do not want to assume they are hiding in the dark. During our last confrontation just outside of our city limits, I noticed many members held personal weapons and bullets. That was the first time they were armed and better able to defend themselves. Up until that battle, many of the rebelling forces were sharing weapons and limiting their use of ammo. That wasn't the case during out most recent interaction with them. Someone is providing them with weapons and I would like to find out who."

I must look as scared and confused as I feel because Logan leans down and whispers so quietly that only the two of us can hear. I avoid turning my head in his direction and just listen.

"All of this must come as a surprise to you. There is

nothing for you to worry about. I will fill you in as much as I can this evening."

I know this is meant to comfort me, but all I feel is the pit growing in my stomach. How many secrets do the Adair family members have that they hide from the rest of our nation? I can't help but feel like so much has been hidden from me my entire life and now I am slowly attaining bits and pieces of crucial information who my parents are, where my locket came from, why Edith has a key that resembles the design of my necklace, who this Legion is, and what purpose it serves. It's all becoming overwhelming.

I hide my discomfort from Logan and slowly nod my head to show my gratitude for his effort to calm me.

The meeting concludes quicker than I anticipated, and when the prince and princess rise, everyone else in the room does similar. Before the soldiers depart, they all bow stiffly and exit rapidly, including Logan, leaving just the three of us in the room.

"David, the whole point of having a companion is so you aren't ever alone. Why don't you ever bring your pet along with you?" the princess spits out.

"I do not need to tow around a person with me to meetings like this one. Instead, I send my companion,

Andrew, to the library to read and study. I prefer to have a companion who can carry on an intelligent conversation as opposed to one who is just a pet like the ones you have trained over the years."

"You think too highly of the lower classes if you really think Andrew is obediently reading in the library. He probably doesn't even know how to read."

"That's enough, Lily. I require you to come to these meetings so you can hear for yourself what goes on in our nation. As you heard, we have to be on constant watch for the Legion. They aren't just fighting us in the Battle Grounds anymore; they are bringing the fight to us right here in Aparthia. We need to be prepared for anything. At the next meeting, please be prepared to offer helpful contribution and advice, rather than scold our soldiers for serving at the frontlines for us."

I can tell this stung the princess by the way her eyes seem to pierce right through the strong prince. Honestly, I'm enjoying every minute of her sting.

"Anyway, let's head to lunch. I am sure the chef has made another delectable meal for us to indulge in."

I peel myself from the wall and attempt to close the gap between the princess and myself. In the process, the prince sidesteps to provide me with room to get by. At this point, I am not certain if he is moving to avoid me because he loathes my presence or if he is acting like a gentleman. I'd prefer the latter, but can't decipher too much about his likes and dislikes just yet.

Another trek to another room. The next time I see Judith, I plan on asking her how many rooms fill this colossal palace. As we glide down one hallway, the prince instructs his sister to wait as he drops off his notebooks in his room. Before he can turn into what I assume is his quarters, his sister tells him to give me the notebooks and allow me to do his bidding for him. That is my job after all. I do as I am told and approach the prince to retrieve the items from him. When I do, I try to avoid making direct eye contact. The prince on the other hand is making every effort to catch my eyes. Just when I reach for the stack of books the prince is grasping on to tightly, I panic and drop one of the books.

The frenzy of me apologizing and bending down to collect the item I dropped begins and rather than lashing out at me, the prince kindly picks up the book and hands it to me. This time, I meet his stare and can't tear myself away. His eyes are just so mesmerizing and calm. I feel myself blush, so I force myself to look at the stack of books and head into his room. I cannot escape fast enough, but when I do Edith greets me just inside the royal chamber. She has been cleaning the prince's room and seems just as flabbergasted to see me walk in as I am to see her. When I am well out of the view of the royal siblings, I find a table to speedily set the books on and grip Edith's arm firmly.

"We don't have much time, but it is so good to see you! I heard you had a mishap with the prince. Are you all right? Is he going to oust you? What does your bedroom look like?"

"Calm down, Elaine. Everything is fine. Yes, I accidentally entered the prince's room while he was in it, but he was kind about it. His companion, Andrew, wasn't as kind to me about it though. As for my room, it is satisfactory, I suppose. How are you?"

"I am losing my mind a little at a time and am beginning to think this whole place is insane. There are so many things we don't know and even more details the Adair family is choosing to keep from us. I don't even know if I can trust anyone in this place. Speaking of which, I need to see your bracelet."

"Elaine, that is something no one was meant to see,

including you. It is just an old family bracelet that my mother gave to me on my sixteenth birthday. She said it was so I could remember where I came from when I had to leave and begin my trade one day."

"I am sorry for prying, but you know the necklace you saw me hiding under my clothing yesterday morning, well, it is a locket. I think your key opens my locket."

"Then take it out and let's see so we can end this madness."

"Elaine! It doesn't take that long to find a table and set the books down. We are going to be late for lunch!" Princess Lily hollers at me.

"I must go, but we have to figure this out. There is something strange going on here, and this might be the first step to finding out who my parents were."

I give Edith a quick hug and return to the waiting prince and princess.

"If I had known setting a bunch of notebooks down would be such a challenge for you, I would have done it myself."

"I am sorry, Princess Lily. I just wanted to be sure I placed them on the best table for the prince to have access to them when he needed."

The princess sticks her nose up and walks on, while the prince watches me closely. One day he is scoffing at me, and the next he is studying me more intently than probably appropriate. He is giving me whiplash from his mood changes.

We finally arrive in the dining room, where the prince and princess sit across from one another. I do not understand why just the two of them need such an extensive table and setup, but it is not my place to question. I look around the room to try to figure out where I should place myself while they eat, when the same disgruntled woman who brought me my dinner the previous night grabs my arm and tows me into the kitchen.

"Your place is here. You are never to be seen during meals unless the princess asks you to stay. Otherwise, you leave her at the table and report to the kitchen immediately."

"Thank you, Ms…"

"Sue. Just Sue."

I position myself at the table Sue motions to and wait for her to provide me with further instruction.

"Well, the food isn't going to serve itself. Get up and pull a plate out. You are welcome to anything set out, as long as it is within reason."

There is so much food to choose from that I don't even know where to begin. I have never seen such extravagant food before, so I don't know what half of it is. I place dollops of just about everything sitting out on my plate so I can taste all of the beauty before me. I grab a seat and take a deep breath before I ensue with the carnage that's about to take place.

The first bite I take is of a warm roll. I have never eaten bread so soft as this before. I just figured rolls were meant to be hard. It tastes sweet like honey - so delicious! Before I swallow that first bite, I am already preparing my next bite on my spoon. It is some kind of soup that I couldn't resist due to the vibrant color of it. I take a sip and sink into my chair. It is so good!

Sue chuckles to herself. "That's spinach and artichoke soup."

I don't even know what an artichoke is, but I love it! The next bite I take is of some kind of meat. Once I take a few hefty bites, I sense the meat is robust and stuffed with bell peppers. Then, it's topped with fresh potatoes, mushroom gravy, and white cheese absolutely divine. Who knew that something so simple could taste so fresh and irresistible?

I must be entertaining the kitchen staff because their

chattering has stopped and many of them are looking in my direction. Sue instructs them to get back to work and reiterates that it is likely my first lunch at the palace. This seems to make sense to the kitchen workers, so they return to their duties.

The final item I grab is dessert. I am torn on whether I should finish my plate of food first or dig into the dessert. Rather than waste more time, I opt to try the dessert. I am not disappointed the second I taste the sweetness on my tongue. It is some kind of peanut-butter pie with a whipped topping and golden flakes on the top. It literally melts in my mouth. I let out a loud exhale and forget where I am.

Once again, I am drawing all of the attention of the kitchen staff. I don't care, though. I am enjoying this meal way too much for any of them to ruin it for me. Yes, it's a heavy meal for lunch, but I wouldn't expect anything less from the Adair family. They appear to enjoy the amenities the palace has to offer and likely wouldn't appreciate a simple sandwich for lunch. Before I have time to lick my plate clean, the princess is summoning me back to the dining room.

"That one always eats like a bird. You better learn how to eat your meals a lot quicker than that if you are going to get good meals in," Sue advises.

I place my dishes in the sink and make my way towards the princess, dejected because I had to leave so much food behind. I'll have to remember to hide some in my pockets the next time I eat in here.

When I enter, the princess is already making haste towards the main door. I curtsy towards the prince and can't help but smile as I bow my head. He returns the gesture, which throws me off balance and cuts my curtsy short. Evidently, the prince finds this humorous and covers his mouth when he snickers. I fly behind the princess and leave as fast as I can out of sheer embarrassment.

Princess Lily and I are on our way to the dress fitting for the Royal Gala when the princess suddenly takes a sharp turn and leads us outside towards a courtyard. Despite the fact that there are guards posted all around the yard since the princess is now out in the open, the view is breathtaking.

"I like to come out here between events on busy days to clear my head."

I didn't think the princess could seem so human, but she does out here. It's almost as though being out here calms her and brings her down a couple of notches.

We are surrounded by an array of flowers and

greenery. I've never seen so many beautiful flowers like this. Frankly, I was under the impression that the battles had left us deprived of sights like this one. There is no need for a roof over this area. The trees are old and tall enough to provide shade for visitors looking to escape. I can identify most of the flowers displayed before me, but only because I have seen pictures of them in textbooks at school. There is a multitude of lilies all around us and I suspect it is because of the princess. She doesn't seem to revere them as I do.

Princess Lily is pointing her chin up towards the sun and slowly spinning in a circle. For a second, she looks just like a child playing outside. This makes me wonder if she ever had the chance to be a child or had to grow up too quick for her to remain innocent and naïve.

"It isn't much, but out here, I feel like I can breathe and just be myself, instead of what everyone else expects me to be."

For the first time since I've been in the presence of the princess I feel a small pang of pity for her. If she feels the need to escape to be herself, I can't imagine what kind of pressure she undergoes on a daily basis. No wonder why she comes off as spoiled - she was robbed of precious childhood experiences.

"Princess Lily, this place is so much more than you realize. It seems to be your haven." I am about to apologize for speaking my mind so bluntly to the princess when she smiles ever so gently at me. This is the first time we have had any sort of a connection, but it doesn't last long. A guard approaches to remind Lily of her dress fitting. Her mask of fearlessness replaces the smile and she stomps out of the courtyard. I trail behind her closely, depressed that I have to leave this hidden gem.

We go through the motions of having the princess fitted for the Royal Gala next week. Everything seems routine for the princess and staff designing her dress, with one exception. King Rennin has requested that I be fitted for a dress as well. According to the seamstress, the king has directed for all women in the Golden Palace to be fitted for gowns so that we may attend. This must be a strategy to begin generating a sense of hope for the women in our nation, step one of auctioning off his son. He will have all of us eating out of the palm of his hand if he provides us with a chance to dress up, something many of us have never practiced in our lives.

Lily completes her fitting, so I am instructed to stand on the podium next. The princess is visually uncomfortable with the fact that the attention has shifted to her meager companion instead of her.

"Get on with it. We have more important issues to attend to than playing dress up with a servant."

And just like that, the connection between us is replaced by jealousy.

The seamstress and her assistants apply all kinds of measuring tools to my chest, shoulders, hips, legs, arms, etc. I think they measured just about every inch of my body. I have never been grabbed and analyzed so closely before, so I stand absolutely still and try to think of the flowers in the courtyard.

"The princess will be wearing an emerald green dress with gold trimmings, so her companion must wear a dress that matches and compliments," the seamstress instructs.

Once the fitting session has concluded, the princess directs me to return to my quarters while she attends a tutoring session for the next hour. I curtsy and make my way to my room, at least I think I do. We have covered so much of this palace today that I am slightly turned around. After wasting close to twenty minutes trying to find my room, I finally identify it purely because I see Logan positioned by the entrance.

Chapter 8

"Good afternoon, Elly. What have you done today? Anything exciting?"

"Oh, the usual, finding out there are all kinds of significant secrets being kept from the people of Aparthia, attending important meetings, gorging myself with delectable food, and playing dress up."

Logan is hesitant to respond, judging by the way he is wringing his hands. "Yes, well, the Adair family does everything they must to protect the wellbeing of our nation and the citizens within it."

Suddenly, I comprehend that Logan is signaling that we are being watched. His words were careful and precise, but his eyes told me something different. I am under the impression that he will explain further when we aren't being observed like we are now. I think back to the cameras in the war room earlier and now fully comprehend what his eyes are telling me.

"I am certain you are correct. It's just all new and a bit overwhelming for me. I must rest while I can before the princess returns."

"Have a nice break, Elly."

I mouth "Thank you" to Logan as I close the door, mostly for warning me about the cameras. To the seeing eye, though, I am thanking him for his polite comment.

If the princess is in tutoring for an hour and it took me a bit of time to return to my room, that means I have roughly thirty minutes to myself. I scurry across my room and nearly knock over my bedside table when I lurch for my bed. My locket is still safely tucked under the collar of my dress. I pull it out and turn it over and over again in my palm. Why would Edith have a key that matches my locket? Why do we share similar features? Is this what Ms. Morrow was trying to reveal to me just before my departure? I must find a way to talk to Edith away from watchful eyes so that I can learn more about who I am. Knowing there is nothing I can do right now, I retrieve the handwritten book that someone left behind on my bookshelf and begin reading.

As I read, I notice this isn't a book at all, but a journal. Someone is recounting days and events in his or her life. Assessing the handwriting and writing style, I assume it is a male who wrote this. How did this end up in my room? I open it to a random page a couple of entries in. I keep reading and fixate on a statement halfway down the page:

"The breadcrumbs left behind for me to follow are hard to decipher. Sometimes I feel like I am on the right track, but other times, I am completely lost. Maybe I was wrong about all of it - about them."

This is exactly how I feel when I think of the locket. I thought I knew who I was, but now since I discovered this locket that Ms. Morrow hid in my waistband, I am so lost, yet intrigued at the same time.

I anxiously begin reading the next line when the princess calls me to her room. She has returned earlier than expected. I place my locket in the pages of the book and gently place the book back on the shelf, disappointed that I have to wait to find out whom this journal belongs to and whom the search is about.

When I enter the princess' room, she has already changed into an athletic outfit that consists of a cropped top, fitted leggings, and running shoes, all dark green in color. To see her out of such elegant attire is strange. I know she must dress appropriately for the task at hand, which is a training session, but I didn't think the princess would actually engage in anything physically challenging.

"You better change, unless you expect to participate in your dress uniform. I must warn you, the workout will be hard as it is, but even more difficult to complete in a dress."

I did not think I would be participating, but this is thrilling. I return to my bedroom and rummage through the clothing someone kindly prepared for me in my drawers and closet before my arrival. I find a pair of black leggings and a loose white shirt with black stripes down the side to match. As for shoes, I find a pair that will have to suffice in my closet. They are definitely nicer than any shoes I have ever worn before. I'm scared to scuff them up. I lace them up and examine myself in the mirror. I might not look like much, but I am content with my selection of clothing.

I return to Lily's room and have to widen my stride to catch up to her as she is already leaving her room. She doesn't seem to wait for anyone.

We arrive in the training facility just a few minutes ahead of schedule. A man who introduces himself as Luke will be coaching us through our session. According to the princess, he trains the Royal Guard to keep them fit and on their toes as well.

We begin with a light jog around the expansive room. I am careful to trail behind Princess Lily so I do not offend her, even though I am dying to break away and run as fast as I can. Once we finish our warm-up, we perform stretches led by Luke. I am estimating he is around twenty, so the fact that he is already training the Royal Guard is quite impressive.

We spend the remainder of the training session completing a series of exercises and engaging in light hand-to-hand combat techniques. I am just starting catch my rhythm when the princess suggests we make things a bit more arduous.

"Now that we have warmed up, let's have a little more fun. Elaine, are you up for a competition?"

The blood drains from my face. The princess will be upset with me if I do not put forth a good effort, yet I have a feeling she will be even more troubled if I beat her. I must tread lightly.

"Yes, Princess Lily. I would enjoy the opportunity to engage in a competition with a woman as fit as you." I can tell by the look on Luke's face that he does not think this is a good idea either. However, he does as he is directed and sets up an obstacle course for us to participate in.

For the first obstacle, we must climb up tethered ropes, touch the top, and then climb back down. The next consists of jumping side to side over a divot in the floor while carrying weights, limiting the use of arms for balance. The third section requires us to run through a virtual reality where people are constantly jumping out at us and attempting to capture us. If we are caught at that point, we lose the challenge. For the final hurdle, we must engage in hand-to-hand combat.

Each obstacle counts as a point with four points total up for grabs. Whoever receives the most points upon completion is the stronger of the two of us. As much as I want to win, I know I shouldn't out of fear of being ousted by the princess in retaliation. On the other hand, I am not built to lose. This should be interesting for both parties involved.

Luke stands tall and prepares to give the signal to begin. The princess looks at me like a piece of meat she is about to devour. Little does she know I've had to fight challenges all my life to survive and get where I am now.

I'm guessing that isn't the case for the princess.

"Ladies, prepare to begin in 3, 2, 1, Go!" Luke shouts.

Just like that, we rush to the ropes obstacle and begin climbing in haste. As proper and elegant as the princess seemed earlier, she no longer seems as such. She is climbing the rope without any signs of a struggle. I underestimated her and she is ahead of me by a significant distance. I use my arms to hoist myself up and attempt to make up for lost time. My pride is faintly bruised when we climb down from the ropes and the princess hasn't even begun to sweat yet. She may have won the first round, but now that I know what I am up against, I will not take situation lightly any longer.

We race to recover the weights Luke identified as the ones we must carry while we jump from side to side over the pit. As we approach the crevices, I launch into competition mode. I clench on to the weight and hop as quick and hard as I can to the left, right, left, right... I refrain from glancing in the direction of the princess in fear that I will lose my focus and balance. It takes about eight good jumps on each side before I am finally done. As I bend down to release my weight, I see that the princess has not completed the challenge yet, but that does not cause her to decrease her intensity by any means. She finishes and casts the weight down as though it were an easy task.

We have to wait for Luke to turn on the simulation before we can begin. This activity is based on whether or not we are able to fight off or get away from the people who will be pursuing us. The princess opts to go first, so I step aside and willingly agree. I am looking forward to being able to see if the princess is as quick on her feet as she is with her snide remarks.

When Lily first enters the system, the room darkens. I can't even see my own hand in front of my face. Suddenly, a figure appears in front of the princess and leaps for her. She is quick to react and dodge his reaching fingers. It isn't that easy to escape from him. He keeps coming for her and she continues to dodge him. It seems the only way to free her from this intimidating man is to fight him. I did not expect to have to fight the system so intensely, so that makes me a little nervous.

A light arises in the corner of the room. Commander Richmond, Prince David, and Logan step forward and position themselves to watch the princess. I am suddenly overcome by a feeling of unease and have to shift my weight back and forth on my feet to keep myself from bolting from the training room. Lily, on the other hand, seems to enjoy having an audience. A smile crosses her face as she clips the man in the chin and knocks him off of his feet, just in time for another figure to arise. This time, the princess has to fight a woman. She strides easily towards the woman and slides right into her, throwing the lady off of her feet. When she does this, another man appears behind the princess and wraps his arms around her. Lily is temporarily thwarted by surprise, but she is quick to recover and stomps on the man's foot. When he jolts back in pain, she kicks him in the stomach and the scenario ends. Princess Lily defeated this challenge without even flinching.

"Well done, Princess Lily-Beth. That is a new personal best for you," Luke announces.

"You become the best when you train with the best," the princess flirts.

"Elaine, you're up. Take your time and keep your head on a swivel at all times. It's all right if you don't absolutely dominate in there. This is your first time and there's definitely a learning curve."

I know Luke means well, but this just makes my heart pitch into my throat. I was nervous before, but now I feel like I'm going to pass out. I step into the simulation and try to steady my breathing.

Before I can get my first deep breath out, a woman that towers over me in size jumps out at me and dives right into my side. I am pinned to the ground before I have time to think about recovering. The woman is about to grab my arms when my senses finally recover. I convulse and roll to the right just as she throws her weight in the opposite direction. She stumbles and falls on the ground. I kick her in the back and begin running.

In my third stride, a man appears and attempts to grab my neck. I am able to dip and avoid, elbowing him in the back as I lean around him. He quickly returns a similar blow to my hip. I dive to the floor and kick my legs and feet up at the same time. As I do, I grab the man and pull him down with me. He disappears and I barely have time to recover when the final figure appears. It is another man and he is sprinting towards me.

This man is massive and his large frame is intimidating, but I notice he seems top heavy. When he reaches out for me, I go low and punch him where no one should ever have to feel pain. He doubles over and I use this to my advantage. I throw my weight on him and try to pin him down. He is much stronger than me and easily rolls me off. He climbs on me and wraps his large hands around my neck. I try to wiggle free, but can't move. It is so strange how this is all in a virtual reality, but I can feel each and every one of the hits and am suddenly struggling to breathe. I'm beginning to see spots and think I'm about to suffocate when I hear the princess chuckle. This instantly wakes me up. I throw my right knee up with all of my strength and nail a hard hit in the man's back. He loosens his grip on my neck and I am able to pull my arms free from under his legs. I clasp my hands and drive both elbows into his face. He disappears and I couldn't be more relieved. It is over.

The lights come back on and the room is silent. After seventeen years of growing up in an orphanage, I have become a master at being scrappy and defending myself. This must come as a surprise to the audience because they are all staring at me with gaping mouths. Luke is the first to recover from his absolute shock. He approaches me and offers a hand to help me to my feet. I oblige and stand tall.

"That was excellent! Well done!" Luke shouts.

"That was pretty good for a first timer, I suppose." The princess cannot just let me have this one. I did way better than even I thought I could do.

I see Commander Richmond and Prince David each

hand Logan something. By the look on their faces, they are not happy to be giving Logan whatever it is. Logan, on the other hand, has a smug look on his face.

"I knew you would conquer that scenario. These other two didn't think you'd be able to defend yourself. Dynamite comes in small packages, right Elly?" Logan says as he winks at me.

The nickname catches me off guard. I still do not understand why I told him to call me that. It also causes stir among the men standing around him. They look at him out of curiosity.

"I knew she could manage, but I honestly didn't see that last one coming. I am impressed and that doesn't happen often," Prince David admits as he turns his focus back to me.

"Thrilling as all of this is, we still have one more round left. As the score stands right now, Princess Lily has two points, which means she is tied with Elaine who also has two points. The winner will be determined after the two engage in a hand-to-hand combat against each other," announces Luke.

My exhilaration is short lived. I completely forgot that I still had one more fight to complete, and it's probably the most important one. I am still trying to catch my breath from the last round and the princess is patiently pacing the floor. Then, it dawns on me. If I win, I will be providing the princess with ammo to oust me. If I lose, the crowd that has come to watch the show will think I am weak. I couldn't be in a worse conundrum.

"If you are ready Princess Lily-Beth, we can begin the next phase," Luke says as he motions towards me.

We walk towards the center of the training mats and begin sizing one another up. I still do not know how I am going to approach this situation. Win or lose, either way I will have to pay in some fashion.

This time, it is Commander Richmond who counts down and signals the start of the fight. Princess Lily plunges for me before I even register the battle has begun. I jump out of her direct line of contact, but she still manages to catch my side. She drives her fist into my side and sends me stumbling. She uses this to her advantage and kicks my feet out from under me. As I fall, I grab her knees and pull her down with me. I try to pin her down, but she hops back to her feet and attempts to kick me in my side. I roll off of the mats and roll right into Prince David. Before I can apologize, the princess is grabbing my arm and dragging me backwards. When I reach for her, she stomps on my hand, which instantly sends pain through my entire body. This is a wakeup call. If I don't start fighting back hard, the princess is going to mutilate me. This isn't just a fun challenge to her. She is coming for my blood.

I elbow her shin hard and pull myself up. As Lily comes for me again, I let her dive down low and thrust my elbow into the back of her head. She hits the floor with a thud and tries to turn over, but I sit on top of her and throw a punch into her spine. The princess screams and lays there in defeat. Just when I think I have won and begin to question what I have done, the princess throws her head back and rams it into my nose. Everything goes black.

Chapter 9

When I wake up, everything hurts. I am terrified to open my eyes and assess the damage. I slowly peel one eye open and then the other. I am struggling to open them widely. They feel swollen and tender. I reach up and try to feel the damage the princess caused to my face - the same face Ms. Morrow thought would get me this job, so that's a little ironic. I got the job but got beaten because of it. If only Ms. Morrow could see me now.

"I wouldn't touch that if I were you," a voice warns from beside me.

I try to sit up quickly, but I am instantly dizzy and guided back down by a gentle hand. When I look around to identify the person who is helping me, I am surprised to find Logan by my side.

"What happened?"

"The princess broke your nose and knocked you unconscious. How do you feel?"

"Like my nose was just broken. How long have I been out?"

"Just a couple of hours. The Adair family is at dinner, so you have been directed to stay in bed and recover as much as you can to be ready for another busy day tomorrow."

Of course… The princess breaks my nose and knocks me out, but she still expects me to be her sidekick at first light.

"Did I win?" I jokingly ask.

"Almost. We all thought you did until she delivered that wicked last blow to your face. Honestly, we were all impressed with how well you were able to fight. Not many companions have ever dared to fight the princess; in fact, I don't think any of them have out of fear of being killed or ousted by her. You have some courage."

"I didn't feel like I had a choice. Plus, I had to show the princess that I'm not as afraid of her as everyone else in this place is."

"Not everyone is as afraid as they seem and she isn't

that bad. She is just really good at putting up a wall and acting the way she must to survive herself."

Logan peers into my eyes as he says this and I feel that familiar connection tugging at me again.

"What would she have to survive against? She is royalty, so I can't think of a single challenge she might have to face, other than which dress to wear to the ball in a few days."

Great. My first ball and I will have a broken nose for the attendees to laugh at. Hopefully, it will turn green enough by then to match my dress.

"More goes on here than you realize."

"You keep hinting at that, but you haven't explained anything further to me. Like this Legion everyone keeps referring to. What or who is that?"

"The Legion is a group of rebel forces that keep attempting to overthrow the Adair power. It is largely composed of individuals who have been ousted over the years. Recently, though, we also found out some of our own Aparthia citizens have been joining in and fighting against us as well. They seem to hide among our people and partake in the Legion only when more forces are needed. In doing so, the Legion has eyes on the inside at all times."

"Have there been battles? Where are people fighting? Have there been deaths? Why doesn't anyone know about this outside of the palace walls?"

"You have a lot of questions, but I think you need to rest. This will be too overwhelming for you to process in your current condition."

"I will not rest feeling like my life is in jeopardy and I don't even know when or why."

"Well, we have been fighting the Legion on and off for about a year now. We don't know why this group is fighting us, other than to overthrow the Adair family. We aren't even sure who is leading them and what he or she wishes to accomplish."

"What about deaths?"

"Yes, both sides have lost a significant amount of lives. For the members of the Royal Guard, their families were notified and paid significant amounts of gold to keep quiet. We did not tell them exactly how they died, but merely that they died protecting the throne. The ones who died as a part of the Legion were already ousted to begin with, so they lacked connections to our citizens in Aparthia."

"What about the citizens who are hiding in Aparthia? Have any of them died?"

"If any of them have been killed, their family members are likely hiding it in fear of being ousted themselves."

"Why hasn't King Rennin informed the public about the Legion?"

"He worries that if it is publicized, more will join the Legion and cause a more significant uproar than we are already experiencing. He also worries the citizens will begin to panic and our system will disintegrate. Classes will refrain from attending their assigned trades, people will start seeking weapons to purchase, and our entire economy could collapse. This isn't something that should be taken lightly, so the king is taking every precaution to ensure Aparthia continues to thrive, even though we are on the brink of another war like the battles years ago."

"You must have some kind of thoughts as to why the Legion has formed and is going through the effort of trying to overthrow the Adair's, don't you? What is worth fighting for and losing lives right now?"

Logan looks like he just might get up and run away from my room. This isn't an easy subject to discuss and yet here he sits, divulging all of this important information to me.

"There are rumors…"

"Yes, what about?"

"It feels silly talking about them out loud."

"Just tell me! You can trust me."

"People are relaying a story about two royal families that lived years ago. There were two princes, one from Anniah and one from Allenthia. Back then, the two nations were sister nations. The royal families of the two shared power equally and had a mutual sense of respect for one another. According to the stories, the Adair family was an outcast, causing Aparthia to struggle on its own. The king at that time, King Gene, was greedy and thought one royal family should rule all three, which the other two nations largely disagreed with. As a result, the two nations signed an agreement with one another specifically stating that they would rule equally."

"When the time came for the two princes to find suitable wives, they found twin sisters, Ellara and Edens, in Anniah. The twins were the daughters of a prominent government official, so both kings approved the selection of them. In marrying Ellara and Edens, the royal families, both Aaron and Ackert, believed this would ensure strong bonds between Anniah and Allenthia. A joint wedding was held and all seemed to work out just as the royal families had hoped, at first."

Despite my lightheadedness, I have perked up and am jumping out of my skin in anxiety.

"Sometime after the wedding, the two queens gave birth to daughters on the same day. The equality among the nations was respected so much that they even planned the births of their children to line up."

That is strange, but I can see how that would work out for the families.

"Not too long after the news of the births spread, King Gene Adair demonstrated his disapproval through an act of war. You see, while the two nations were happily celebrating their growing royal families, King Gene was building and prepping an army for invasion. The royals of Anniah and Allenthia never saw this coming from King Gene. They knew he was bitter and wanted more power, but they never envisioned he would cause a war out of pure ambition. Now, this is where the details get a little hazy."

I still feel dizzy as I listen, but not because of my injury. I am flooded with unease as I listen to this story.

"That's fine. Just tell me anyway. My curiosity is eating me alive," I almost shout.

"Apparently, the royal families were tipped off about

the onslaught that was about to occur, just before King Gene's forces reached the palace perimeters. They made an agreement to send off their daughters, who were just a couple of months old, to keep them safe and ensure their royal bloodlines continued."

"The confusion lies in whether the queens were successful in getting their children to safety or if they were killed in the battles. According to King Gene, he ensured all of the royals were killed off. However, many say the queens smuggled the girls into Aparthia knowing the king would not look within the borders of his own nation for them."

"They were brought here? I don't understand."

"King Gene wanted all to believe he was flawless and an impeccable leader. If he tore his own nation apart to find two children who wouldn't even know who they were when they were older, he would truly look ambitious, yet weak. That is why he told the citizens of Aparthia that he killed the two royal families personally. To this day, no one knows what really happened. King Gene was killed by Allethian forces on his trek back to the Golden Palace, so he never returned home. Members of the Royal Guard are sworn to the Adair family, so they would never risk their lives or the possibility of being ousted to say otherwise."

"So, you're telling me there could be two princesses in Aparthia who don't even know who they are? That's the saddest story I have ever heard," I quietly say.

"If it's only a story…" Logan trails.

"What do you mean? You told me it is a story based on rumors."

"Well, that would explain why King Rennin made changes to the choosing ceremony procedures this year. All of that was seventeen years ago, so those babies would be turning seventeen this month, which means…"

"They would be starting their trades."

"The king must have some doubt that his father really killed all of the royal family members or he wouldn't be going through the trouble of overseeing this month's ceremonies."

"…Or he knows something we don't."

How do I even begin to process this? My whole body is shaking. If this story is true, there are two princesses among us who have no idea who they really are or where they came from. If, on the other hand, they do know who they are, that would definitely be grounds for another war.

"Like I said, it's all overwhelming and a lot to digest."

"It is, but that would explain quite a bit, like the

choosing ceremonies, the sudden uptick of the Legion, and the royal family's constant desire to have the Royal Guard secretly watching the citizens and positioning undercover guardsmen in the neighborhoods."

"It would make more sense, but it is all just a story, Elly. You are overthinking all of this."

"Maybe I'm just piecing all of it together so it makes sense."

"I think this is enough story time for tonight. You need to rest up so you are ready for Princess Lily-Beth's demands in the morning."

"I suppose you are right." I don't want Logan to leave, but I need time alone to process all of this. Plus, I have this strange feeling like that journal propped up on my bookshelf has something to do with the newly divulged information.

"Dinner is on your side table if you get hungry. Sue whipped up something that smells wonderful. If you need anything, I'll be just outside the door for a few more hours."

"Thank you, Logan, for trusting me enough to tell me all of this."

"Thank you for listening. Goodnight, Elly."

"Goodnight, Logan."

As soon as he closes the door, I am out of my bed

and flying towards the bookshelf. Before I can reach it, I am overcome by the room spinning around me and have to return back to my bed. I suppose Logan is right. I need to recuperate tonight and pick this up tomorrow.

I can't even think about eating right now, despite how wonderful the food smells. I climb back into bed and fall asleep almost the moment I hit the pillow. My dreams swoon of my locket, the journal, and what the queens looked like. All of it seems so mysterious and appealing.

Chapter 10

When I wake up, the sun is just beginning to rise over the peaks of the distant mountains. I spring from my bed and begin the ruthless activity of getting ready for the day. My head is spinning and the pain of my nose is agonizing. No matter how much makeup I apply, my black eyes and even darker nose cannot be concealed. I opt to avoid applying any eye makeup since the darkness circling them already draws in enough attention as it is. Just when I have finished, I hear the princess calling for me. I hurry to her room and glance around the room for her schedule of events for the day, without looking in the princess' direction. I'd rather not give her the satisfaction of seeing the damage she caused to both my face and my pride.

"She lives!"

"And so it seems, Princess Lily."

"I did you a favor. You are much more attractive now than you were before I broke your nose. Maybe your nose won't be so pointed once it heals."

"If only I could be so lucky. Forgive me for being bold, but after everything you went through yesterday, how do you still look so flawless?" I can't see a single bruise on the princess. Not to toot my own horn, but I am certain I caused some damage to her, yet there is no proof of it.

"You didn't lay a hand on me, Elaine," the princess teases as she winks at me.

Lily tosses a small jar of something towards me. I catch it and wait for her to tell me what she would like me to do with it.

"The miracle of good medicine. Take two every four hours and you will feel and see a difference by tonight."

I am pleasantly surprised that the princess is willing to share her medicine with me and cast a small smile in her direction.

"I'm not doing this for you. I just don't want you to detract the attention away from me at the dance in a few days. The medicine will speed up the healing process so you don't look so terrible, although I do like seeing the damage I caused."

The pleasant surprise has now been replaced by sheer shame and regret. I should have crushed her when I had the opportunity.

"Not a single one of my companions has ever agreed to fight me, but you did. Why? What makes you so different from all of the other companions I have had over the years?"

"May I speak frankly, Princess Lily?"

"That is why I asked you."

"I did not think I had a choice. I worried that if I turned down your request, you would have had reason to oust me. Likewise, if I did fight you and win, you would have been able to oust me then as well. It was a no win situation for me, so I chose the route I wanted to choose. I desired to show you I am capable and tougher than I look."

The princess eyes me with suspicion, but she does not scold me. Instead, I see a glimmer of a grin spread across her face.

"You are correct. I could have ousted you for either decision, but I am grateful you chose to go with your better judgment. For the first time in a long time, I had a fair challenger. It was fun. Let's not make a habit of it, though.

I did not enjoy attending dinner without my companion by my side last night. Plus, if we were to fight again, I am confident you might not wake up after."

The last part serves as a warning, not just a statement. Princess Lily is warning me not to overstep myself because she is quite capable of taking care of me with her own bare hands.

Today is full of more meetings, dress fittings, meals, and tutoring sessions. Before we begin carrying out our duties, I slip back into my room to take some of the medicine the princess shared with me. I am reaching for a glass of water when I am startled by a knock at the main entrance to my quarters. I quickly digest the medicine and head for the door. Before I can even reach for the delicate knob, the door is swinging open. Andrew is holding the door open for Logan and Prince David to enter with the companion, Andrew, pulling up the rear.

A knot forms in my throat. Maybe they are here to punish me for my fight with the princess yesterday. She was the one who knocked me unconscious, so I technically lost the friendly competition. I throw myself into a curtsy and wait for someone to speak.

Prince David is the first to address me. "I just had to

see it for myself. Logan informed me that you are alive and well, but I wanted to be certain."

Since when does the prince care about the wellbeing of a companion? This is truly strange.

"Was my sister kind enough to share her precious hoard of medicine with you or did she keep all of it for herself?"

"She shared out of her worry that I would diminish the attention for her beauty at the Royal Gala. Thank you for checking on me. Is there something else I can help you with, Prince David? Forgive me, but I find it strange that you came all the way to my quarters just to check on me."

"You are right. I also came to see how my sister is fairing. She isn't accustomed to someone actually putting up a good fight against her. Has she woken up from her much needed beauty rest yet?"

I hear Logan laugh and then act as though he is clearing his throat. I find it humorous to watch the way these two interact. When they are together, they act like children.

"She is. I believe she is preparing to depart for her full day of activities as we speak."

The two men head for the adjoining door, but Andrew hesitates and stays behind.

"Do you need something, Andrew?" I ask.

"I saw Edith this morning. She asked me to check on you. She is worried about you."

"Please tell her I am fine. Barely a scratch on me," I say with a halfhearted wink.

Even blinking hurts, so I'm not sure why I thought winking was a wise idea.

"She also asked me to relay a message."

"Yes, go on."

"She will be cleaning Prince David's chambers while he is at dinner this evening. She thought you should know."

"Did she say anything else of importance?"

"That was it. Just asked me to inspect you and relay her schedule of cleaning to you."

"Oh. Thank you for that, Andrew."

I suppose this means she wants me to try to meet her there if I can get away from Princess Lily during that time. As Andrew exits the room, I retrieve my locket from the journal and place it around my neck. The high collar of my uniform hides it from eyesight, so I should be able to contain it just in case I am able to meet Edith. I am hoping she will have her key on her as well.

When I enter Princess Lily's room, she is obviously

very annoyed with her big brother. He is dancing around and teasing her about something I haven't caught on to yet.

"Just because you think you can fight now doesn't mean you are ready to play with the big boys, sweetie," the prince chastises.

"Let's see what a sweetie I am at training tomorrow, or are you too afraid to fight a girl?"

"I am not afraid to fight anyone, especially my little sister."

"You have such a big mouth, but such a little brain," the princess says with a smile.

Logan clears his throat and the prince stands still. When he looks my direction, he straightens out his shirt and fumbles with his words. I realize my nose is striking at the moment, but I did not think it would deter the prince this much.

Princess Lily is watching the scene and does not like what she sees. "There you are, Elaine. I thought you were going to be quick. It seems I must explain what being speedy truly means before this becomes a habit for you."

"I am sorry, Princess Lily. I had a spot on my uniform and was trying to clean it up." I am getting better at lying, but that isn't necessarily a good thing.

"Yes, well, we better be on our way then. We don't want to be late for our meeting with the Royal Guard," Prince David interjects.

Everyone vacates the room and we make our way towards the dark war room once again. Now that I know a little more about who the Legion is, I am anxious to hear if any updates have developed over the last twenty-four hours.

We enter the room and everyone takes the same seats they had yesterday. Likewise, I place myself against the wall with Logan by my side.

Prince David begins the meeting. "Commander Richmond, have there been any new developments since we inserted more undercover soldiers in the neighborhoods?"

"Yes, Prince David. The neighborhood guards are reporting whispers of dissention among many of the citizens. Apparently, the Legion is attempting to recruit new members right under our noses. They are spreading false hope, but citizens in the lower classes are starting to follow them. We do not know how many exactly, but we did notice a small uptick in traffic in the Battle Grounds early this morning before the sun rose. People seem to be crossing through there in larger numbers than usual. We are also seeing more tents sporadically set up throughout."

I didn't even realize people stayed anywhere near the Battle Grounds, let alone lived there. If Commander Richmond is saying citizens are joining the Legion, there must be some truth to the rumors Logan told me about.

"How do our numbers compare to the numbers you are seeing in the Legion?"

Commander Richmond pauses before he answers, obviously choosing his words meticulously. "Sir, it is hard to tell how many are now in their ranks, but based on the little we can see, we should have substantially more members of the Royal Guard than they have in the Legion. However, it would benefit us if we could expedite the training of the soldiers who were recently drafted into the Royal Guard so that we can add a significantly larger group of soldiers to our frontlines."

"Very well, Commander Richmond. Make it happen. If that is all…"

Logan clears his throat and it seems this gesture was meant to signal something to Commander Richmond.

"Actually, Prince David, there is more. Officers are also reporting more sightings of weapons, some of them we have not yet been able to identify."

"What do you mean there are weapons you can't identify?"

"The information we attained leads us to believe the Legion has been able to get their hands on new weapons that we are not familiar with. Based on their appearance, they are a sort of bomb, but we do not know exactly what they do."

"Commander Richmond, I am disappointed you did not bring this to my attention sooner. This is not something that should be taken lightly or held back from any member of the royal family. That goes for you too, Officer Price. You were by my side all morning and yet, this is the first I am hearing of this."

The commander and officer lower their eyes and nod in unison.

I can tell by the smug look on Princess Lily's face that she has a plan.

"Offer a reward to anyone who can provide more information on these newly found weapons. Spread your own whispers of the reward as being paid in a large sum of gold to the first person that comes forward with accurate details. You are all dismissed."

Princess Lily seems quite content with herself at the moment.

The crowd rises, bows, and hastily exists the room. I'm not sure why, but there is suddenly a heavy feeling enveloping the room.

"Do not be so bold as to exercise your power over mine. You do not dismiss the Royal Guard - I do. You will inherit that right if you ever become the queen."

"Settle down, David. I was only trying to help you. The commander just dropped his own bomb on you and you needed to find a way to control the situation better. I did that for you."

I can tell by the look on David's face that he is about to tear the princess apart.

"Excuse me, Prince David and Princess Lily, but if we do not get on our way now, we will be late for our next appointments."

The pair shoots me a look of disbelief and silence. Someone had to interfere before the situation became even more hostile than it already was. I am waiting to feel the wrath of both of them. Instead, the two seem to grasp my intention and slowly depart from the room. Andrew, Logan, and I trail behind.

As we reach the doorway, Logan meets my gaze and reveals a look of approval. The men head for another meeting of their own and Princess Lily and I head for our second dress fitting. When we are alone, she seizes the opportunity to push me back into my place.

"Do not ever interrupt a conversation between my brother and me like that again. You are my companion, which means you should be seen and not heard, unless you are addressed first. I should oust you for your intentional show of disrespect."

"Yes, Princess Lily. I apologize."

"That being said, I appreciate your effort in defusing a potentially hazardous situation. We are both stubborn and arguments between us are never easily resolved."

The princess is biting her pride! I never thought I would live to see this day. It must be the medication she is on. Maybe it is causing her to settle down and be nicer to those around her. Actually, now that I think of it, my nose is feeling notably better.

We go through the motions of the day and attend all of our scheduled events. Dinner is quickly approaching and I still haven't been able to conjure up an excuse for why I cannot attend dinner so that I may slip away to meet Edith in the prince's room. I am absolutely dying to see if her key opens my locket.

"Elaine, what exactly are you thinking about that is more important than me? I have called your name three times."

"Forgive me, Princess Lily. I was just realizing that I do not know how to dance and the Royal Gala is just a few days away."

"Well, stop thinking about yourself and think of nothing but me for the moment."

"Yes, my lady. How may I be of service?"

"I asked you what you think of the Legion. As a citizen from a lower class, what would draw you in to them? Why would they even have cause to rebel against their king and queen? I am asking direct questions, so I expect direct answers. Do not tiptoe around this like you usually do when I ask you important questions."

I am speechless. With everything else that has been going on, I had not thought about this at all. Why is the Legion growing in number? What could have caused it to form in the first place? I take a minute to think before I open my mouth to respond.

"I suppose people just like to feel included in the

decision-making process. As it stands, lower classes do not know anything about what goes on in the government and royal house. We just go along with the expectations that have been set forth for us by others. We are rationed when it comes to basic necessities, such as food, electricity, and hot water. With such limitations, many of us are forced to go hungry and go about filling our needs in manners that are not approved by neither the royal family nor the Royal Guard. There is also the matter of marriage. We do not feel like we can marry for love; instead, we marry higher up so we can gain rank. The Golden Palace has never felt such turmoil, so we would not expect your graces to understand where we are coming from."

"Is that all, Elaine?"

"I am not done, Princess Lily." I am seizing the opportunity to talk to her as she talks to me. It feels good to cut her off.

Still, it is becoming evident she did not really want an honest answer when she asked me these questions. Maybe I am divulging too much, but if she is asking, her curiosity is forcing her to learn hard lessons she should have learned long ago.

"There are also rumors involving the other two royal

families from Allenthia and Anniah long ago. People are beginning to question the honesty of King Gene. Some believe the royal daughters still live among people of Aparthia. Others believe the king did kill the girls when they were babies, so there is division."

"I do not see how this would cause stir among our citizens."

"If people believe two other royal family members are still alive, that means they also think there will be more battles among us, even greater than before. Two nations would rise up and fight against us, likely killing many citizens in the midst of it. Allenthia and Anniah would want their queens back and the rest of us would be caught in the middle of it. Ultimately, citizens dislike the fact that they have been lied to all these years and are tired of being ruled by a family who keeps secrets from them. If the Legion succeeds before the other two nations have the opportunity to do so, they might be able to prevent a larger battle from taking place and destroy us all."

"Is this how you feel, companion?"

I wake from my concentration and realize I have been mindlessly saying my thoughts out loud. Honestly, at this point, I am not sure what I believe. So much information has been distorted and much of it is all based on rumor. Who really knows how to digest any of this?

"Of course not, Princess Lily. I am assuming a great deal and do not even know if any of this is plausible as to the reasoning behind the Legion's existence. Besides, I am basing these assumptions on bits and pieces of details I have heard."

"That reminds me, how do you know about the rumors of the young queens from Allenthia and Anniah?"

I process the severity of what I have just done. Logan confided in me and I turned around and opened my mouth to one of the few people I should not have discussed it with. I try to recover as best I can.

"Other girls were talking about it in the room next to mine the night we were brought here and I overheard them. They were also relaying rumors they heard at their school. My guess is they were trying to ease their nerves by dishing on the latest gossip around town."

"Interesting," is all the princess can say at the moment.

Now, I am not sure where we stand. I not only revealed my true thoughts, but I also gave the princess fuel to begin picking apart strengths of the Legion. Currently, I am not certain if this is a good or bad thing yet.

Dinner is quickly approaching.

"Princess Lily, may I be excused to retrieve more medicine from my room? The nose you shattered is beginning to cause great pain."

"Oh go ahead and be weak. I no longer need you this evening anyway. Retreat to your bedroom for the night."

That was easier than I thought it would be. I depart and travel down the intricate hallways to my designated room. I do need to take more medicine and prepare myself for my meeting with Edith.

Chapter 11

I take my medicine and look at my reflection in the bathroom mirror. The princess was right about the medicine being efficient. I do look and feel so much better in comparison to my appearance and state this morning. We never had access to medicine like this in the orphanage so I really didn't believe anything like this existed until I saw the jar for myself this morning. Actually, I highly doubt any citizens other than government officials have been able to appreciate the healing impact of this medicine. I clutch the necklace around my neck and prepare for my departure. On the way to my room, guards do not seem to pay attention to me. Really, there is no reason for them to on my way out either. They will just assume I am heading to dinner with the royal family since that is where I am expected to be anyway.

I ensure my locket is safely tucked away under my uniform and make my way down the elongated hallway once again. When I reach the end of the way, I must choose whether to go left towards the dining room or right to Prince David's room where Edith is waiting for me. The nerves in my stomach are pulsing, but I go right anyway. If any of the guards question me, I will simply act lost. It is easy to get turned around in this large palace, so I am sure they will believe me when I lie to them through my teeth.

As I round the final corner to the prince's room, Logan steps in front of me and catches me by surprise. "Elly, where are you heading at this hour? Aren't you supposed to be at dinner with the royal family?"

I was prepared to lie to any of the guards, but Logan is a different story. I am not sure where his true alliances lay, but I do feel a sense of trust between us. I decide to take my chances and tell him the truth.

"The princess excused me so that I may take more medicine and relax for the evening. She no longer required my service."

"That was very kind of her. May I escort you to

wherever your final destination is then?"

"Well, I am going to Prince David's room. Before you ask why, I need to know that I can trust you."

"You can trust me with anything."

The sincerity in his eyes tells me I can believe him, but, I'm not even sure how to explain any of this to him. Instead, I ask him to come along with me. When we arrive at the prince's room, Logan opens the door for me. We enter and see Edith hastily making the prince's bed.

"I didn't think you were coming. We are almost out of time. Did you bring the…"

Edith just turned around to face me and laid eyes on Logan for the first time.

"Why did you bring him? We could be ousted for even having the items we possess! I trusted you!"

"It's alright. We can trust Lo…Officer Price."

"How can you be so sure? He is an officer in the Royal Guard, which means he reports directly to the commander and the Royal Adair family."

"I just know. We confide in one another."

I slowly turn to face Logan. He relaxes his shoulders a bit and nods at me.

"Miss Edith, you can trust me with whatever is going

on. I may be an officer in the guard, but I am also a human being outside of my hours of duty. Right now, I am off the clock and was on my way home when I ran into Elaine. I do not mean to make you uncomfortable."

He stares into Edith's eyes with that same familiar intensity that even she begins to falter in his presence.

"Hurry up, Elaine. The prince will be back any minute," Edith says with her eyes still on Logan.

I quickly pull the locket out from the confinement of my uniform collar. The beautiful piece of jewelry is so vulnerable and precious. Edith unfastens her bracelet and holds it out for me to grab. Before I insert the majestic key into the clasp of my locket, I take a deep breath and attempt to regain my composure. Suddenly, I am frightened about what I might find once I open the golden locket.

"Elaine, whatever is in your locket, we will make it through together. If it is something we don't like, we go on about our lives and pretend we never saw it. If, on the other hand, it is something positive, we pursue that course hand in hand. Plus, the key might not even fit. We will not know anything until you try."

Edith and Logan step in closer, eager to see if the mystery key fits and what the locket has to offer our curious eyes. I hold the key up and insert it into the lock of my necklace. At first, it doesn't turn. Then, Edith grabs my hand, steadies it, and turns the key in the opposite direction.

"Click!"

The locket opens and I hold my breath. On the right side is a picture of an older man holding two very young babies. By the look of the picture, it was taken during a happier time long ago. The man's grin is massive and the babies each have little pink bows on the sides of their heads. One has ahold of the man's white beard while the other seems to be asleep. It is an adorable sight. On the opposite side of the locket is a quote.

"To the ones we love the most - never forget where you came from. From two small seeds grow fields of flowers and beauty, just like the two of you will do. With all of our love, EA"

I am stunned. Edith must be as well because she has yet to say anything. We take a minute to study the picture and inscription. Neither one of us recognizes the family in the picture, nor do we know who EA is.

Logan glances at his watch and alerts us that the royal dinner should be concluding by now.

"I don't understand any of this," I confess to Edith.

"Neither do I. I don't even know who that family is. Could we be related to them somehow? Who is EA?"

"I wish I knew, but Logan is right. We need to get out of here before our jewelry is discovered and we are ousted for sneaking around like this. We will have to meet up again soon so we can figure out what all of this means."

The three of us make our way to the door. Before we exit, Edith gives my hand a firm squeeze.

"See, we are no better and no worse. At least we know we are connected somehow," Edith says confidently.

"I appreciate your positive outlook, but I think we are definitely way worse now. We have been given very vague and limited information that we likely won't even be able to sort out. How will we ever get any closure on this?"

"Someone is bound to know something about who EA is and the identity of that family."

Logan squirms just enough for me to notice. "What do you know that you aren't telling us, Officer Price?"

"I do not know anything. I was just thinking…"

"Spit it out! We are running out of time!" Edith raises her voice.

"If the initials are EA, that means whoever owned that locket and had it inscribed was a member of a royal family.

Only the royal family has a last name that begins with the letter A."

I hadn't even thought about that yet. I was fixated on the design of the locket and just having a piece of jewelry like this. I never really considered the actual letters or pieced it together.

Edith speaks first. "If that's true, that means someone we know stole this jewelry from the royal family. I don't even want to think about my parents having any involvement in this."

"…Or someone in *a* royal family gave it to them to give to you two. What are the odds that two girls of the same age would have matching jewelry pieces and would come together to figure it out? Small, I'd say," Logan points out.

"I don't like the way you emphasized *a* royal family, not *the* royal family," I respond.

"That's because I'm implying that it's possible these pieces came from one of the other two royal families years ago before King Gene Adair murdered all of them."

The room is spinning. I need to lie down. This is way too much to process and take in at the moment.

There is commotion coming from down the hallway so Edith closes the chamber doors and departs one direction and Logan and I the other. As we make our way down the hall, the prince comes around the corner with Andrew in tow.

"Officer Price, Elaine, where are you two going? I thought the princess mentioned that you were retiring to your bed for the night, Elaine."

This is it. I'm about to open my mouth and confess everything.

"Prince David, Miss Elaine took her medicine and it made her drowsy and lightheaded due to a lack of food. We didn't want to interrupt your dinner, so I thought it best to take her around to the back of the kitchen for some food."

The prince looks to me for confirmation.

"Yes, Officer Price happened to be on his way out when I stumbled upon him. He has been kind enough to try to find a way to make me feel better. That medicine is quite powerful."

I can feel my cheeks begin to flush, but I am unsure if I'm blushing because I'm lying to a member of the royal family or if it is because the prince seems to know just how to look at me to make me nervous. I will say the way he looks at me now is a significant improvement in comparison to how he looked at me the first time he laid his eyes on me at the choosing ceremony.

"Very well then. See to it she eats so she is ready for another busy day tomorrow. Lily will eat her for breakfast if she is not perky and prompt in the morning."

I curtsy and Logan bows before the prince makes his way passed us. Andrew, on the other hand, winks at me as he walks by. In an odd way, that gesture is more comforting to me than he knows. Maybe our explanation was believable after all.

Once the pair is behind a closed door, I let out a loud sigh, just long enough to realize there are cameras all over this palace. I'm suddenly choking on my own air and dying from the inside out. Logan grabs my shoulders and turns me around to face him.

"Act normal until we make it back to your room. We can talk then."

With quite a bit of effort, I do as he suggests and we finally arrive at my bedroom door. The walk back could not have been more excruciating. We close the door behind us and I collapse on my bed.

"I forgot all about the cameras! I can't be ousted. There's no way I'll survive in the Battle Grounds. They are going to have to force me to take one of those pills. Either way, I'll be dead by morning."

I'm in full panic mode when Logan begins to laugh.

"I'm sorry - is the thought of death funny to you? I asked you to go along with me, so now you're just as good as dead as I am. Poor Edith! She doesn't even know about the cameras. What have I done to all of us?"

The tears are streaming down my face and I can't stop them from pouring out. I ruined all of our lives for a dumb necklace.

Logan is rolling in laughter now and I am ready to punch him in the face.

"Logan, if you don't tell me what you are laughing about, I'm going to…"

"Whoa! Slow your roll with the panic and drama. Do you really believe I would have gone along with you to the prince's bedroom if we were being watched? I can be dumb sometimes, but that would really take the cake."

"What are you talking about? You're the one who told me about the cameras in the hallways and main rooms."

"We perform routine maintenance and updates on the cameras once every two weeks. Tonight was one of those nights, which means the cameras have been down for about an hour now. No one was watching us."

Now, I am crying even harder out of relief. This seems to confuse Logan and make him uncomfortable. He shifts his weight and begins eyeing the door, planning his escape.

"So we aren't going to die? That's great news! You could have told me that a lot sooner instead of allowing me to have such a dramatic meltdown first."

"It's getting late. You really should get some rest. Prince David wasn't joking when he said the princess will eat you for breakfast if you aren't on your toes in the morning. I should be heading home anyway. You aren't the only one who has an early morning tomorrow."

"I suppose you're right. I have to wake up extra early every morning to make myself halfway presentable to the princess. That takes more effort and energy than you realize."

"One more thing - thank you for trusting me to go along with you and be a part of whatever this is."

"Thank you for being someone I can trust. It is nice to finally have someone around me who I can rely on. I didn't have much of that growing up."

"It is my pleasure. Goodnight, Elly."

"Goodnight, Logan."

When he makes his way towards the door, I can't help

but smile at him when his back is turned. I haven't been able to put my finger on it yet, but something about him makes me excited and nervous at the same time. Between him and the prince, I am constantly on edge and unsure about myself.

An hour later, I finally complete my bedtime routine and I am just exhausted. I briefly consider pulling out the journal and reading a few pages, but decide against it since I will likely fall asleep in the process and wouldn't be able to put it out of eyesight if someone were to enter my room unexpectedly. I opt to go to sleep instead.

I am just about to doze off when I suddenly have an epiphany. I shoot up from my sleeping position and frantically turn on the light next to my bed.

How did Edith know the cameras would be off at that specific time this evening? How did she even know about the hidden cameras? Based on the information Logan has provided me with, not many know they are being watched within the palace walls. Could it be a coincidence that she asked to meet during that exact timeframe, or did she just think no one would notice and we would be able to get away with it?

Something about this doesn't sit right with me. Edith

either knows more than she leads on or she is braver and more careless than I thought.

I spend the rest of the night tossing and turning in bed. So much for resting tonight. I get up twice to take more medicine and use the bathroom. Each time, I can feel a pit growing in my stomach. I have so much to figure out about the details surrounding the locket. I am also wondering about Edith and what she does and doesn't have knowledge of.

Chapter 12

The next few days come and go in a blur. Before I know it, the night of the Royal Gala is upon us. Thanks to the wonders of the medicine the princess gave me, I am no longer hideous due to the bruising of my broken nose. In fact, the bruising can be easily covered by makeup and can no longer be noticed by the naked eye. Instead, I am merely unsightly because of the rings under my eyes, which concealer is not so willing to hide.

Since the night Edith and I discovered our jewelry is a match, the two of us have not crossed paths. I still have a turning feeling in my stomach and wake multiple times a night due to my unease of the entire situation. During the day, I cast those thoughts aside and carry on with the dauntless duties that come with the trade of being a companion to the princess.

We have been preparing for this ball, which has consisted of sending me to multiple tutoring sessions with more people than I care to name. I have been taught how to eat like a lady and walk in a dress and high heels. Additionally, I was forced to learn basic dance steps so that I can participate in the less complicated dances, not that anyone is going to ask me. Lily was worried that I would embarrass her if someone did happen to ask, so she made sure I could get by for at least a few songs. If someone asks me to dance to a song I do not know how to dance to, I am to excuse myself to the restroom, strictly specified by the princess.

Princess Lily has Jackson's styling team in her room preparing her for the ball, while I have another team of two women dressing me in my room. The main stylist, Emma, keeps wrinkling her nose at me in dissatisfaction. I guess I'm not as polished as she would like me to be. The two women work quickly and have me ready just in time for the princess to inspect me and make certain I am groomed enough to stand by her side throughout the ball. When I enter her royal bedchamber, she is simply breathtaking.

Surely, it will not be hard to go unnoticed in the presence of Princess Lily.

Her dress is sleeveless, fitted through her torso, hips, and thighs, and then just before it touches the ground, it spreads out into a fan. The green of her dress reminds me of pine trees that spring up around our town during winter months - deep and rich. Specs of gold glitter are embedded throughout the attire, making the entire gown mesmerizing. The most striking detail of the elegant dress is the minute, but bold, fan on the bottom. That entire section is shimmering gold, and when the light catches it just right, it looks as though it is made of pure gold. There isn't a soul in the palace that will not be captivated by Lily as she enters the ballroom.

The duration of the time I am studying the princess, unbeknownst to me, she is doing the same to me. I must not look too appalling because she looks pleasantly surprised.

My dress is green like the princess', but just a shade lighter. The neckline is v-shaped and connects to sheer gold sleeves that puff up in all the right places. While the torso of the dress is fitted like a bodice, the gown shoots out at the hips and flows as I walk. Unlike Lily's dress, mine is gold all the way through the bottom and possesses a lucid gold layer on the surface to add just a touch of gold glitter. Thankfully, I learned how to walk in heels in recent days. Otherwise, I would trip over my own feet and surely ruin the masterpiece of a dress Jackson created for me.

"I see Emma was able to demonstrate her skills as a miracle worker. You look beautiful, Elaine. The boys would be silly not to ask you to dance."

That has to be the nicest compliment the princess has ever given me, maybe even the only compliment.

"Thank you, Princess Lily. Jackson didn't have to work very hard on you. You are stunning as usual, but truly glowing this evening. The attendees won't even notice me with you by my side." This seems to make the princess blush and she looks down to avoid sincere eye contact.

"Alright, let's get on with it then. I am ready for this night to be over. Elaine, lead the way."

Usually, the princess enjoys all of the attention focused on her, but she seems a bit off this evening. When we enter the ballroom, we step onto a long black rug that runs from the main entryway to the throne the royal family is perched on. Princess Lily and I are the last to arrive, so the room grows quiet when we take our first steps onto the black rug, which nicely contrasts the gold woven through our gowns. I take my place behind the princess and wait to be announced.

"People of Aparthia, I present to you Princess Lily-Beth and her companion." Just companion. No name. We stride down the black runner and I keep my chin down for most of the walk to ensure I do not trip and embarrass the two of us. When we finally reach the throne steps, I look up momentarily and see the prince and Logan looking at me. While Logan nods his head in approval, the prince just stares. His reaction is hard to read, but he does not look too dissatisfied. I fashion a humble smile and redirect my gaze to the king and queen. They are grinning at Lily with such love and admiration that the entire room seems to melt.

Finally, the princess takes her seat on the throne and I stand just out of view behind her. The music begins and the crowd closes the walkway to dance. I look around the room to see if any of the other companions and servants feel as pretty as I do at this very moment. I have never had an opportunity to dress like this before, so I am quite enjoying myself. For the first time in my life, I feel truly beautiful. Then, I see Judith and Edith just across the way from me. Edith is wearing a lovely gown that fits her all the way through, with a slit that begins at her hip and doesn't stop until it touches the floor. She looks jovial and content. Judith, on the other hand, is wearing a very loose fitting gown and looks extremely uncomfortable. She looks right at me and I take her look as a jealous response. I'm not sure what I have done to deserve this look, but she looks absolutely furious with me.

Luckily, the princess offers me some advice, which forces me to break contact with Judith. "Elaine, something you will learn very quickly is many of the men here are only here for attention. Therefore, they will only ask you to dance if they think it will benefit them somehow. Just watch the men who ask me. None of them want to enjoy my company. They just want people to see them dance with the royal family. Choose your suitors wisely so you aren't taken advantage of too much." I assumed this initially, but hearing the princess say it out loud suddenly makes me realize why she did not seem too thrilled to attend this evening. She does not want to be used as a showpiece.

The evening goes on and Lily has danced with several different men, including her father, Logan, the commander, and Luke. The only difference between them is the way she looked at Luke as they took a spin around the room. He seemed to make her cheeks redden slightly and they talked the entirety of the song. Luke looks at her with such intensity and interest. Maybe there is a connection there. It is sad to think that connection will be broken when she begins her travels to find a suitable husband from one of the other two nations. I do not envy her position.

My thoughts are interrupted when Logan approaches and asks me to dance. "Would you like to see if your dance lessons were worth the time?" He hitches his elbow up and I gladly take it. Of all the people to dance with, I think Logan is the best option. He makes me comfortable, so I am not too nervous to try my hand at dancing. We walk to the main floor and a song I recognize begins playing. He pulls me in close and leads the way. I don't even hesitate to follow.

"Ah, I see the time you put into lessons worked. You have only stepped on my foot twice."

"I barely touched you. For such a tall man, you apparently can't handle much pain," I say with a grin.

We make our way around the room and carry on light banter the entire time. We argue like we have known each other for years. Conversation flows naturally with us and I am enjoying every minute of it. When the music stops, we part ways and I return to my post by the princess, who seems to have taken the last song to rest her feet.

"Be careful with that one. He is very calculated and knows exactly what to say it and when to say it." Before I can press the princess on what she is referring to, she is asked to dance by a gentleman and she gladly accepts.

"Miss Elaine, would you care to dance with me?" The deep voice echoes in my ear and I instantly stiffen out of apprehension.

"Prince David, I am honored." I take his outstretched hand and follow him to the main floor. Everyone seems to part and make way for the prince. They appear just as stunned as I am to see the two of us together. With all of the distractions of the evening, I hadn't even noticed whether or not the prince danced with anyone else. The music begins and he places his strong hands on my hips. When I don't instantly respond, he says, "You are supposed to put your arms around my neck for this one." Somehow, this makes me relax enough to do just that and place my arms awkwardly around his neck. I instantly feel his neck muscles flex in response. That humors me and I feel a chuckle arise in my throat.

"What do you think about all of this? It's a little extravagant, isn't it?"

"The two of us dancing? It is a little overwhelming."

"I was referring to the Royal Gala. It must all seem so foreign to you."

"Oh, right. It is like nothing I've ever experienced before, especially the whole wearing a fancy dress part, although I kind of like it." This makes the prince grin.

"I haven't quite figured you out yet. Some days, I think you are appalled by me and other times, you act like I don't faze you at all. Which is it?"

I can't help but laugh as I respond. "That is exactly how I feel about you. The first time I saw you, I could tell that you were physically repulsed by my presence. You even described me as a companion who would be unsuitable for you. Our brief interactions between that first meeting and now have made me dizzy. Sometimes, I feel okay around you, while there are also instances when I am waiting for you to oust me at any second."

"That is just my nature. I make every attempt to be a good human being, but there are times when I let my royal upbringing get the best of me."

"You mean when you act entitled?" This really throws the prince for a loop. I don't think anyone has ever been so upfront with him. He stops dancing and looks like I injured his pride.

"If you think I am entitled, you don't know anything about me."

"That's just it - I don't."

Prince David looks around the room and sees people are beginning to stare at us. He inhales and begins leading me around the dance floor again. "It seems we have a lot to learn from each other then."

We continue a light conversation for the rest of the dance, and go different directions as soon as the song concludes.

My head is spinning from the nerves raised by the situation and I spend majority of the remainder of the ball scrutinizing the details of our conversation. Just before the last song begins playing, the king informs the guests of his plans for his children in the coming months. Lily is to travel to Allenthia and Anniah to form better relations with the citizens, while David will soon begin his search for a wife in Aparthia. He glosses over the details to avoid providing any guidelines or specifics for now. Instead, he watches the crowd for reactions. I do the same and see Edith and Judith perk up. The king has just provided many of the women in the room with a very small glimmer of hope that they might have a chance with the prince. It really is a great strategy. For now, this keeps many of the citizens on the king's side, which might discourage some of them from joining the Legion.

My feet ache from wearing heels and I make my way toward an empty chair. Before I reach my desired destination, an older man I do not recognize steps in my direct path. "Miss Elaine, would you please have the last dance with me?" I am tempted to reject his offer, but do not want to offend the man. I nod and follow him to the dance floor for the last time. We pass by Edith who is dancing with Logan and she eyes us suspiciously.

We spend a fair amount of time swaying in silence until the man has guided me to an area where not many are around us.

"It seems the king has many plans for our nation. He has always been an opportunist." This comment seems strange and I attempt to dodge it.

"Yes, he is an excellent strategist. We are lucky he is our leader."

The man squints his eyes and squares his shoulders. "Are we, though? Lucky to have King Rennin as the leader of our nation?"

I panic and violently search for someone within earshot of us. Talking about the king like this could have both of us ousted, or worse - killed.

"Listen quickly before anyone else approaches us. I need your help with something, but before I discuss my desire with you, you should know I am the one who gave Ms. Morrow the locket and instructed her to give it to you on your seventeenth birthday. I know who you are and who your parents were. There is much I can tell you of your past, but you must help me first."

He can see that he has my full attention now. I stare at him with wide eyes, vaguely aware that we are still dancing to the beat of the music slowly. There is something faintly familiar about him to me, but I cannot identify what or how. "What can I do for you, Mr...?"

"Kenneth will do and I will tell you all about your family if you will provide me with some much needed information. I believe you know of the Legion, right?"

I slowly nod my head in disbelief that this man has the audacity to talk about them in the Golden Palace.

"Well, I represent them and we need to know where exactly the princess will be traveling, how long she will be there, and what the true reason for her travels is. You should know that we have no intention of causing any harm to her. We just need to piece together why the king is suddenly rushing to strengthen ties with the two other nations he has had little to do with ever since the battles years ago."

I am willing to sacrifice everything to know who I really am and where I came from, so I agree, with one expectation in return. "I can get you that information, but first, I need you to tell me more about the Legion. Why are you really fighting against the royals and government of Aparthia? Are any of the rumors true? I need to know I am helping something greater, not risking my life for a group who represents a cause I do not believe in."

Kenneth takes this into consideration and then constructs a careful response. "It is simple. We seek freedom like our neighbors. There are no classes there and they are free to rule themselves. Yes, the Royal Guard regulates them and the king appoints government officials to carry out his orders, but he leaves them relatively alone as long as they do not cause problems for him. We also hope to avoid another battle that will tear all of us apart like it did many years ago. Too many lives were lost then and we aren't willing to pay that price again. Another driving factor for us is the matter of information the king hides from the citizens of Aparthia. We know for a fact descendants of the royal families of Allenthia and Anniah are living here in Aparthia and we have plans for them."

The music has ended and guests are departing. Abruptly, Kenneth tells me he will contact me in a few days to retain the information he has asked me to identify for him. Then, he flees for the exit before I can generate a response to him.

"Who was that man you were just dancing with?"

I turn to face the princess. "I am not sure. He mentioned owning some sort of business, but we did not get into details."

"You two talked a lot for not getting into specifics."

"We were only commenting on the beauty of the palace and the kind gestures the king will be exercising in the months to come. It seems the citizens are excited for the upcoming changes. We will all benefit from your travels and your brother's marriage to one of our own."

Princess Lily doesn't look the least bit convinced, but she tightens her jaw and avoids pressing me further.

Instead, she keeps her eyebrows raised and says, "I see. Let's go to bed. It is late." We head for our rooms and remain quiet along the way.

After a tumultuous bedtime routine, I finally climb into bed and fall asleep quickly, exhausted from all of the overstimulation from the events of the day. The next few weeks will be interesting, to say the least.

Chapter 13

It's been two weeks since the Royal Gala and I still cannot stop replaying my conversation with Kenneth over and over again in my head. I am desperate to know about my family, but also greatly intrigued by his comments about the other two nations experiencing a freedom I have never known before. Marrying whomever I choose and not having to worry about class separations has never even been a consideration on my part. More importantly, if what he said about royal family members living in Aparthia is true, a battle is upon us with or without the Legion's assistance. Either way, if the circulated rumors are true and the young princesses do not know who they are, they will soon find out with the whirlwind of information slowly beginning to make its way out in the nation. Then, our neighbors will have no choice but to fight to reclaim power over their own nations.

"I didn't believe it was possible to pack any slower than you have been the last couple of days, but you are testing that belief as we speak. We leave in two hours, so put a little more effort into it."

The princess has been growing more and more irritable towards me the last two weeks. She doesn't like that I did not tell her what Kenneth and I were discussing at the ball and has been demonstrating her dissatisfaction with me ever since. She did not give me the schedule of events for our trip until yesterday, even though she has had it in her possession for the last five days. At this point, I am doing all I can to regain her trust. If I want to survive in this position, it is all I can do to avoid being killed or ousted.

"I just want to be certain you will have all you need for a successful trip. You can never have too many outfits. Besides, we have to assume various events will be held in honor of your presence. You will need to bedazzle them as you have the citizens of Aparthia, especially any potential suitors that we may come across." I was trying to earn back the princess' favor, but struck a nerve with the last part instead. I couldn't resist it, even if it wasn't the wisest decision I have made today.

"Do not pretend to be anxious about meeting any suitors. We are going to avoid them as long as we can."

"But hasn't your father already sent word ahead to his assigned government officials that you will be in search of a future husband during your travels? They will likely be discouraged if they arrange to have their finest men meet you and you decide to avoid them. Their efforts must not go unnoticed if you are making an effort to establish relations with their people." I do sincerely mean what I am saying. We must tread lightly if we hope to have any success during our travels. Additionally, if the princess meets someone who rises to her daily games and challenges, this will likely take a considerable amount of attention and pressure off of me.

"When did you become so wise? You do make a valid point. We will only avoid until we are directly approached on the subject. Otherwise, we carry on and get to know all we can about our friends. This isn't just your first time outside of our Aparthia, but mine as well. There is much for us to learn about the people, their economical build, and the layout of the nations. I have spent years seeing pictures of the mountains and only viewing them in the distance on clear days. I am looking forward to seeing them in person."

Up until this very moment, I always assumed the Royal Adair's were well rehearsed in visiting Allenthia and Anniah. I suppose only Prince David and King Rennin have had reason to make their way into those areas. This is the first time I have been able to think of the prince's name without it stirring some sort of feeling in my stomach. Nerves? Embarrassment? I'm truly unsure at this point. Based on our conversation during our dance a couple of weeks ago, neither one of us hate each other, but we also lack much knowledge of who the other person really is. Some small part of me was hoping to be one of the women that will be attending events at the Golden Palace in the coming months. Prince David's own pursuance for a future queen is beginning as well. However, with our trip to Allenthia and Anniah taking place during the same time, I will likely miss out on a significant portion of that, even though I do meet all of the guidelines and expectations set forth by the royal family. I suppose all of this is irrelevant anyway. When I agreed to provide Kenneth with the information he was seeking, I was giving up the chance to really become close with the Adair family. Some days I regret that decision, but those days are outweighed by my lingering desire to find out who I really am; that means more to me than securing a lifelong position as a companion in the palace.

When I finish packing for Princess Lily, I return to my room to ensure I have packed all I need for myself as well. I look around the room and opt to grab the journal from the shelf and the locket from my bedside table. The trip to our first stop in Allenthia is estimated to take roughly two hours, so I should have time to myself to read the journal and relax just a bit. I place the two items inside my suitcase and make my way to the door. When I reach for the knob, I cannot turn it. In fact, the door seems quite stuck. I panic and throw my weight into the door, just when the prince does the same on the opposite side. The door flies open and we knock into each other hard. I do not even comprehend who the figure is until I look up to scold the person for momentarily trapping me. I am startled when I meet the prince's eyes, especially because I am awkwardly entangled with him at the moment.

I jump to my feet and attempt to recover. "I am so incredibly sorry, Prince David." I am in utter shock.

"No, forgive me, Elaine. I did not mean to make you fall. The door was stuck and I was trying to get in. Now I see that it wasn't actually stuck."

The silence is building, but I do not know what to say. It seems the prince is just as stumped. He aimlessly glances around my room before he finally speaks up.

"I just wanted to wish you safe travels on your trip. Lily tells me you will be leaving shortly."

"Yes, I was just retrieving some last minute items before I catch the train." It seems like the prince is holding back from saying something and we are running out of time, so I decide to prod him just a little.

"Is there something else, Prince David?"

"Well, I mostly came to tell you that the final list of acceptable women for me to meet arrived this morning. As I read through the names, I saw one I recognized."

At this point, I am certain he is talking about me.

"Why didn't you tell me you would be on that list?"

"I suppose with everything going on recently, it just slipped my mind," even though it didn't. I honestly wasn't sure how the prince would feel about it or if it would even matter to him.

"With your travels going on at the same time as the suitor events, you will not be able to participate. However, with your permission, as well as my sister's, I would like to send for you to return to the palace temporarily so you may engage in the occasions."

I can tell this was hard for the prince to admit, but I am thrilled he is even making this an option for me. "It would be my pleasure to attend if it can be arranged."

"I just want to make sure every qualified woman has the same opportunity." Just like that, the specialness I felt seconds ago disappears. He just wants to be fair to everyone. I should have seen that coming. My face must show my disappointment because the prince continues.

"It is also my desire to get to know you better. I only know the little you have been willing to show me, so if I am going to make arrangements for you to attend, I need to know you are going to open up more and let me get to know Elaine, not the companion she represents."

My smile gives me away before I can respond. "I can do that."

"Then it is decided. When the time is right for you to return, I will send for you."

"That sounds like a plan to me."

"Very well then. I should see my sister off and ensure this plan is suitable for her as well. Have a safe trip, Elaine."

"Thank you, Prince David. I am looking forward to our next meeting." I really hope that doesn't sound too cheesy, but I can't hide the sudden excitement building within me, at least until I think about my conversation with Kenneth.

Everything is so confusing right now. Kenneth hasn't reached out to me for any of the information he asked me to acquire, so it's possible he changed his mind and no longer requires my aid. If that is the case, though, I might not ever know about my past.

We board the train and are dispersed into several different train cars, each one prettier than the next. I select one that is void of any Royal Guards and take a seat next to the window. Princess Lily is gossiping with her stylist crew in the car over, so she will not notice my absence right away. I take a minute to scrutinize my surroundings and appreciate the glamor of it all. The walls are lined with colorful satin that shines in the sunlight and all of the furniture is covered with some sort of fur. The centerpiece of the car is a large wooden table with six chairs surrounding it. I am guessing the purpose of this car is to serve as a meeting room.

The designers really thought this one out. There is a car for meetings, one for dining, another for lounging, three for sleeping or overnight stays, a workout car, and one for training simulations, just to name a few. Extravagant doesn't even begin to describe the decorations within each of the cars. Each one has a different theme to match the purposes they serve. The meeting room has fur everywhere to provide a hunting vibe, the workout car has images of start and finish lines, the sleepers have clouds and stars painted on the ceilings, the kitchen car is decorated with old cooking equipment and pots and pans, and the training car has screens on all sides for simulations. Absolutely overdone in every way.

Before long, I settle in and begin reading the journal I brought with me. It is hard to keep focused when the thoughts presented are so jumbled and mixed up. I don't get very far in my reading before I am puzzled again.

"Today is my fourteenth birthday and the gift I received from the people who I thought were my parents was to tell me that I was, in fact, adopted years ago. How can this be true? They claim I was found wandering the streets of Allenthia alone when I was three years old, so they took me in and waited for someone to come looking for me. When no one did, they decided I was meant to be a part of their family. As hard as this was for me to hear, it explains a lot. I look nothing like my siblings and parents who all have dark features and are more round than I am tall. I always wondered where my blue eyes and blonde hair came from, but just assumed someone way down the line of our family had the same features as me. At least I know the truth now. It only took them eleven years to share it with me. I pressed them for more details and they said they didn't have anymore for me. No one knows where I came from or how I ended up here. I have to know more about where I came from, so I am going to talk to the man I have known to be my father all these years. I suppose I should just call him Kenneth until I find out who my real parents are. I'll wait until the only mother I have ever known falls asleep and then corner him into feeding me more details.

Did I mention my parents also gave me this journal to record my thoughts in? I suppose they thought it would be helpful for me to write out what I'm feeling as I navigate my way through all of this."

Kenneth! The man's name in the journal is Kenneth. That is not a very popular name around here, so it has to be the same Kenneth I know. Plus, it makes sense. This story is taking place in Allenthia and Kenneth said he isn't from Aparthia, which means there are only two other options. I keep reading, eager to know where this tale is going. I am not disappointed when I read the next entry.

"Kenneth seemed hurt that I addressed him so

formally. I suppose he has been a father to me all these years, so I should cut him some slack. All he had to offer was that I wasn't actually lost on my own, but with him the entire time. Apparently, someone stole me from an abusive home and gave me to Kenneth so I could have a chance at a happy life. The emotions from all of this are suffocating me. When I pushed for more information, Kenneth just said I came from Aparthia and he thought it best I didn't know who I really was so that I wouldn't try to find the people who neglected me as a child. Part of me is appreciative, but the other part wants to know where I came from."

I know exactly how this person feels. I can't stop myself from reading the next few entries. The first couple of writings continue to discuss how torn the author is about whether or not he should pursue a course of action to identify his parents. Then, the third one shifts gears.

"The more I read at the library, the more I am learning about the history of our three nations. I am convinced I fit somewhere in Aparthia, but I haven't quite figured out where. Kenneth is starting to leave me breadcrumbs so that I can find out where I came from on my own. I am certain he knows exactly who I am and where I came from, but he is unwilling to tell me. He thinks I will put all of the pieces together when I am ready to accept the whole picture and carry that burden with me. I wish he would just make it easy for me.

In the library today, I read the story of two daughters of the queens of Anniah and Allenthia. Over the years, it has been said that they were murdered, along with their parents, but the textbook I found here in Allenthia suggests otherwise. Someone wrote a very detailed book suggesting the queens in Anniah and Allenthia knew the battles were about to begin, so they found a way to keep their children safe by sending them to another nation where they could live out their lives until it was time for them to return and reclaim their rightful thrones. I know this is farfetched, but I think I am somehow linked to this story. I was three years old when the battles took place and was found just days after they concluded. There has to be some connection there."

So it is true then. The princesses survived and were delivered to Aparthia. So how do Kenneth and the narrator fit into all of this? I am about to find out the answers to my questions when someone gently raps on the door. Emma walks in and has a seat next to me. I slowly close the book and attempt to turn it on its side so Emma can't get a good look at it. We sit in silence for just a minute until Emma seems to work herself up to the reason she came in here to begin with.

"An acquaintance of ours has asked me to recover some information from you. He said you would have the schedule of events and outline of the travel plans in your possession. Do you have them on you?"

I am speechless. How could Emma possibly know Kenneth? Maybe this is a test from the princess. I am calculated when I respond. "I'm sorry, but I think you have me confused with someone else. I don't believe we share any acquaintances."

"We do and if you want to know about your locket and family history, you will give me what he has requested." Right to the point. I shouldn't have expected anything less from Kenneth or Emma it seems.

I retrieve the outline from my pocket and hand it over. She doesn't even open it. She just stands to leave, until I stop her.

"I was promised information in return. When will he keep up his end of the bargain?"

"You will know more soon. When the time is right, he will plan a run-in with you and explain then."

That's it. She leaves before I can ask anything else of her. Emma is way more interesting than I thought she was. I mean, she is a great stylist, but now she has connections to the Legion. How can this be? I am starting to see how the Legion has been growing in numbers and attaining vital information. They have spies embedded in the Golden Palace. This makes me turn my attention to the journal again. Maybe it will divulge more information about Kenneth so I can know something about the man I am risking so much for. I read the next entry. It is the part I read a few days ago, so I just gloss over it.

"The breadcrumbs left behind for me to follow are hard to decipher. Sometimes I feel like I am on the right track, but other times, I am completely lost. Maybe I was wrong about all of it - about them. I know the princesses who would now be queens are alive, but I cannot track them yet. I am certain finding them will tell me who I am. I will keep looking."

Over the course of the next year, the narrator continues his search and studies. He doesn't seem to find anything worthwhile until he discovers Kenneth's personal journal tucked away in an old trunk.

"Kenneth has been lying to me all this time! He

knows exactly who I am and what happened to the princess babies. He is the reason I am living with a different family in Allenthia. He took me away from my real parents in Aparthia out of retaliation for King Gene killing the royal families of Allenthia and Anniah. When he comes home from his nightly indulgence of alcohol tonight, I will corner him and get it all out of him."

This is insane! Kenneth stole a child and kept him as his own son for years. He also knows what happened to the royal children. For some reason, I feel sick to my stomach and have to take a break from the book. After seventeen years of leading a pretty mundane life, the last few weeks have more than made up for any dull moments I experienced growing up. All of this newly discovered information is going to make my head explode. I couldn't even stand up right now if I wanted to. Instead, I decide resting my eyes and sleeping for just a little while would be good for me. I close my eyes and drift off into a deep sleep.

As I sleep, I dream of the locket and the people inside of it. The man with the beard looks so familiar, but I can't place him. I am searching for him in my dream, but he keeps avoiding me. Where is he going? Why can't I catch him? When I finally touch one of his shoulders and turn him around, he is smiling at me. He is also holding the locket and telling me the time will come when I discover who I am. Just then, I bolt up.

The man in my dream is Kenneth, but Kenneth is also the man in my locket! I can't believe I didn't realize it before. When I saw Kenneth at the Royal Gala, he was clean shaved and sported a cropped haircut, probably due to his involvement with the Legion. In the picture in the locket, he has longer hair and a beard, but I am certain it is the same person. How is Kenneth so involved in all of this? I reach for the journal again and drum my fingers on the armrest of the chair as I continue reading. My thirst for more answers and connections is relentless.

"I did it! After quite a fight in the main room of the house, I was able to pin Kenneth down and make him talk. It is his fault for spending so much time on teaching me how to properly defend myself. According to Kenneth, my real name isn't Logan. My birth name is Thomas."

Logan! I should have known. The description of being tall with blonde hair and blue eyes should have triggered some kind of recognition in me, but it all makes sense now. This is Logan's journal and he must have left it in the room for me to find. I still don't understand why he meant for me to find it, but I know that was his plan. I keep reading   for more epiphanies to come to light.

"I wasn't in an abusive home at all. In fact, I was a member in the Royal Adair family in Aparthia. Kenneth stole me right out of the courtyard while the king and Royal Guard were busy fighting the battles. My mother never even saw him sneak in and snatch me up. No one directed him to take me, which is why he never told anyone, including me, who I really am. He was on a mission from the Aaron and Ackert families to deliver the two babies to safe houses in Aparthia when he generated his own plan. I know I should be furious with the man, but I just don't understand any of it right now. For now, I am getting out of the house and avoiding any contact with Kenneth until I am ready to process all of this."

I don't know if I am going to scream or pass out. Neither would be a good idea, considering the princess is in the car right next to mine. I am having a hard time processing all of this myself. So, Logan isn't actually Logan. His real name is Thomas and he is the big brother to Prince David and Princess Lily. He is the son to King Rennin and Queen Majorie. So why is he still posing as an officer in the Royal Guard   and why hasn't he revealed his identity to his real family? I don't understand any of this. Of course I would find out all of this information when I am nowhere near Logan or Thomas, whatever his name is, to punch him in the face and get more out of him.

When I turn the next page to continue reading, the rest of the pages are blank. This is absolutely crushing. I have just learned that the person I have trusted to listen to me bash the royal family is actually part of that same family. He has been keeping this huge secret all along and patiently waiting for me to find out in a book that he left unfinished. How does any of this make sense? I can't even function right now. All I can do is sit and stew in the fact that I have been betrayed. This should make for an interesting trip to Allenthia.

On second thought, this should make every day thought provoking from now until I find the answers I need, especially to one very important question I have yet to find the answer to - how do I fit into all of this? I was so wound up about learning who Logan really is that I hadn't considered my place in this mess. Why did Kenneth give Ms. Morrow this locket to give to me? I have a feeling these questions are going to take me down a road I can never be truly prepared to travel down.

Chapter 14

When we finally arrive in Allenthia, we are in the largest city of the nation called Portencia. Judging by the banners waving on the entrance to the train station, it is referred to as The Port. We are soon greeted by a Royal Guard representative and the assigned governor of the nation, along with a posse of their own. The group bows and curtsies as soon as they see Princess Lily appear in the doorframe of the train car. She motions for them to stand and makes a grand entrance down the steps of the train, which are also paved in gold. These people spare no expense when it comes to their flashy decorations and amenities.

"Welcome to The Port, Princess Lily-Beth. We are honored to have you visit us. I am General Dell Reese, but

Dell will do just fine."

"And I am Shara Betancourt, assigned to regulate this section of Allenthia by your diplomatic father, King Rennin."

The princess eyes both women like bugs that need to be squashed. I know that look well. Lily looked at me like that the first time she saw me and on and off again since then; it depends on the mood she's in. She smiles anyway and nods in approval at the two. "Thank you for having us in your great nation. We are excited to see the vast mountains and spend time with the affable people of The Port." She waves at the crowd as she says this and they erupt with cheers. This is the first time they have seen the princess in person and their reaction says it all.

"If you will follow me this way to the transports, we will head to the palace and get you settled in before dinner."

The mention of a palace surprises me. "I didn't realize you all had a palace here as well."

Dell smirks at me and says, "Of course, child. Did you really think we would let the Aaron palace go to waste? We inherited it after the battles and did some decorating of our own. It now serves as Allenthia's headquarters for meetings and events."

Dell is an older woman, but is obviously not one I would mess with. She has salt and pepper-colored hair that is styled in tight braids that wind into a solid bun in the back. Her broad shoulders and toned arms inform any who lay eyes on her that she is a fierce woman who can match any who oppose her.

Shara, on the other hand, sits in stark contrast to her company. She is in her thirties and vibrant in every way. She has gorgeous light brown hair that cascades down to her waist, golden eyes, tan skin, and a thin frame. Judging by her flawless outfit, she leads a pampered life. Being a government official under King Rennin must pay well enough to keep her more than comfortable.

Princess Lily rides in a gaudy black transport decorated with gold trim and Aparthia flags on the front of it. Meanwhile, I am in the lead vehicle with Dell and a few members of the Royal Guard that traveled here with us. We are riding in a plain black transport that doesn't look any different from the Royal Guard vehicles in Aparthia. This is my first time riding in a transport, so I embarrassed myself by shrieking earlier when the engine roared to life. That seemed to amuse Dell more than I would have liked. Jackson and Emma's styling teams are in the third vehicle back and another Royal Guard transport brings up the rear of the caravan.

Many people line the streets and try to catch a glimpse of the transport with the gold trim, knowing the princess must be within it. I could be wrong, but there seems to be a mix of reactions arising from the crowd. While some are cheering and clapping, others are standing back, devoid of any emotion. I suppose I wouldn't be too happy to see the royal family who overthrew my own either.

"It's nothing like Aparthia, but the king is good to us here. We have all the food and supplies we need and the people never cause a stir. It's a simple life for simple folk."

"But if there aren't any classes, how does any work get done? How do people know which trades to pursue?" I know this is a bold question, but I've been curious ever since Kenneth put these thoughts into my head.

"It isn't too different from the practices of Aparthia. After the battles ended, many of the families who were already working in trades stuck with them. At that point, it was too hard for them to start over and do something new. Then, their kids carried on the same trades and so on. We do occasionally have people who choose to venture out and try their hands at new trades, but it is hard to find someone who is willing to train someone new to the trade since they could become competition. People still try to marry someone who has more to offer than they currently have on their own, so really, even though the names of classes are gone, that structure still remains so to speak."

I'm not sure if Dell is saying this to convince herself or me. When I study the reactions of the other Royal Guard members, they don't seem swayed in the slightest either. We spend the remainder of the drive in silence, which provides me with much desired time to observe my surroundings. The city is a little older and could use some updating, but it is in relatively good condition. The streets are clean and the buildings stand firm. I expected the city to be in much worse condition considering they don't have a royal family actually living in the nation to oversee it. I suppose that is Shara's job.

After a short drive, we arrive at the palace that once belonged to the Royal Aaron family. It is beautiful. Unlike the Golden Palace, this one seems more reasonable. It isn't flashy or overbearing in the slightest. Instead, the focus of the construction seems to have been fortitude and resilience. It's too bad it didn't seem to do them any good during the battles. I presume it's a demonstration of different priorities with the various royal families years ago. Where the Golden Palace possesses gates made out of it's very name, this one has gates that have been wide open for years. They are also small and appealing. Maybe that is where they went wrong. I do not see any evidence of a way to fasten the gates closed, so they must have been welcoming to their citizens and not so worried someone would attack them.

When we get inside, we are dispersed to our bedrooms. Instead of an adjoining room, the princess and I have rooms right across the hall from each other. Considering Lily hasn't been awarded the luxuries she is accustomed to in her own palace, she is actually doing a pretty good job of hiding her disgust. I have only seen her grit her teeth twice and both of those times were when Dell and Shara were far enough ahead of us not to notice.

With an introductory dinner taking place this evening, the princess and I get to work with our styling teams. I request to be on the simple side of makeup and attire, but Emma huffs at me and continues with her own plan. There is no mention of our run-in that took place on the train just hours earlier. The fact that she is a part of the Legion, but still a worker for the Adair family continues to confuse me. How has she made it this far and not been identified? How was she even recruited in the first place?

When the styling team has finished preparing me for dinner, they depart and I make my way to the princess' room. She is also ready and her team has vanished. We are rarely alone, so I take this opportunity and use it to my advantage.

"Princess Lily, how well do you know Emma?"

"I don't make it a habit to get to know servants, so I don't know her well at all." I should have figured as much.

"One thing I can tell you is she isn't one to be trusted." This is exactly what I was looking for.

I try to find some common ground. "She does great work and I appreciate how she is able to hide my flaws and make my appearance more suitable, but there is something about her that doesn't sit well with me." This seems to peak Lily's interest and further engage her in the conversation.

"Remember when I suggested we pay people to provide us with information on the Legion?"

"Yes, I remember. That was a very good idea, not that you need my approval."

"I know it was a good idea because it worked. Emma came forward not long after the announcement and provided us with some crucial information. She was able to tell us about the new weapons the Legion is currently utilizing, as well as where they are coming from."

I knew it! Emma isn't on anyone's side. She is only thinking of herself. Not only is she giving Kenneth information to provide the Legion with, but she is also betraying that relationship by getting paid to give the Adair family information about them in return. I can't blame her for doing what she can to survive, but her methods are dangerous and questionable.

"If she is providing you with such important information that benefits Aparthia, why do you say she cannot be trusted?"

"Someone who has to get paid to bring us such information is a traitor in my eyes. She should have come to us before we offered money. Besides, this tells me she has alliances elsewhere, which is how she attained the specific information she delivered."

This is a valid point. It is only a matter of time before Lily grows tired of Emma and ousts her when she no longer provides information that can be used to the Adair's advantage.

We leave for dinner and have to find our own way since there isn't a plethora of servants around to guide us. This seems to irritate Lily, but we eventually find the dining room by following the growing volume of chatter. We are announced upon our entrance and Lily takes a seat at the head of the table. When there isn't a seat right next to her for her companion, I find an empty seat quite a ways down from the princess and situate myself. I wasn't sure whether or not suitors would be at this dinner, but judging by the large amount of young men seated all around the princess, I now understand Shara opted to have her most handsome men attend in the hopes of catching the attention of princess. The only other two women close to the princess are Shara and Dell. What an excellent strategy.

Halfway through the meal, I hear laughter erupt that I am not accustomed to and look up to witness the princess engaging with a very attractive man. He must have said something absolutely funny because I have never seen or heard the princess laugh like this before. That, or she is playing a game and dominating it. I grin at her and return to my meal, but when I do, I instantly lose my appetite. Kenneth has positioned himself directly across the table from me when the woman who was previously sitting there excused herself. How did he even get in here?

"It's nice to see you, Elaine. How have you been?"

"Well, these last few days have been interesting, especially the last four hours when I was able to catch up on some light reading. Do you know how Thomas is doing, by the way? I haven't seen him in a couple of days now."

The mention of Thomas makes Kenneth shift uncomfortably in his chair. He looks around to see if anyone is listening to our conversation and calculates his response.

"I have not seen him in a few months, but I hear he is doing well." Of course he doesn't regularly interact with him, but there must be some kind of communication between the two. Figuring out how much they touch base is crucial. These days, I have no idea who I can and cannot trust.

"Did you receive the information you were looking for?"

"I did. Thank you."

"That means you owe me some information in return."

"My dear, that is why I am here - to hold up my end of the bargain." I don't like the way he is condescending towards me, but I smile and look on anyway.

"Would you like a tour of the castle?"

I still do not think I can trust this man, but I have risked my life to give him the princess' schedule for the very information he is willing to give me now. "I would love one. Thank you."

When we rise to leave, I look over my shoulder and see Princess Lily is flirting with the men around her too much to notice my departure. We walk quietly for a few minutes until we reach a cosmic room that appears to be a library. I have never seen so many books in my entire life. Kenneth leads me to a fireplace and perched just above the mantle is a large painting. My throat catches and I feel tears streaming down my face. I recognize the baby in the picture. In this picture, though, the most gorgeous woman I have ever laid my eyes on is holding her. There is also a dashing man standing with his arm around the waist of the woman, while he is touching the forehead of the baby at the same time. Even though the features are so much more enhanced and elegant on the woman, I would recognize them anywhere. Dark eyes, pointed nose, high cheekbones. She is breathless.

"Is this them?"

"I figured it would make more sense to show you rather than tell you." He isn't wrong, but I still have so many questions.

"Why hasn't this painting been removed yet? I figured

every trace of them would be gone by now."

"It serves as a reminder of our past, but also as a warning. We stay in step or we are gone, just like they were."

"Was it easy for them? To say goodbye?"

"You mean, was it easy for them to send you away? Of course not. In all my years as your mother's father, I had never seen or heard her cry like that before."

Kenneth has just said more to me in one sentence than others have said to me in a lifetime. The man standing next to me is my grandfather and the people in the picture are my parents. As for me, I am Elaine Aaron, princess of Allenthia.

"When do we start?" I ask as I clutch the meaningful locket hiding around my neck.

"Start what, my dear?"

"Taking back what is rightfully mine."

Chapter 15

When we return to the dinner, Princess Lily is clearly enjoying the attention the attendees are giving her, especially the suitors. I approach and ask her if she is ready to retire for the night. She doesn't even look up to acknowledge me. Instead, she just waves me off and continues with her childish giggles and flirting. I suppose that is how women of her caliber grasp the attention of men. I hope I never look that silly around men. Then again, I don't have the opportunity to flirt or giggle because I am too busy embarrassing myself by literally falling into them.

By the time I find my way back to my room, I can feel the taste of bitterness forming in my mouth. I spent years starving and stealing to survive. I also grew up thinking

I was unloved and abandoned when I shouldn't have had to go through any of that. Now that I know I am one of the long lost princesses people are talking about, I cannot sit idly by and not take what is mine. There are so many factors to consider at this point. When I pushed Kenneth for more details, he only told me what he was willing for me to know during our brief interaction.

Evidently, Edith is the other princess that was rescued from the battles years ago. Kenneth is our grandpa and he knew questions would arise if two babies randomly showed up together and on the same night. As a result, he painstakingly left me on the orphanage doorstep and gave Edith to a relative of his. I still don't understand how he chose who to place where and why he just left me to suffer at an orphanage, but at this point, I'm just grateful to be alive and finally know who I am. According to Kenneth, Edith still doesn't know who she is and he thinks it should stay that way for now, at least until we have a solid plan.

Our tentative plan is for me to be ears in the Royal Adair family. During my travels with Princess Lily, I am to carry on and let Kenneth know if major changes or updates occur...through Emma, which I am not thrilled about. I asked if I could relay messages through Logan (Thomas), but Kenneth doesn't think I should tell him that I am aware of any of this yet. The less who know I am essentially awake, the better.

When we return to the Golden Palace, I am to pay attention to every detail in the briefings with the Royal Guard. Meanwhile, Kenneth is going to continue recruiting for the Legion and finalize weapon negotiations. Up to this point, weapons have been stolen piece by piece from a secret armory in the Aaron palace. The only ones who were aware of the emergency stash were members of the Aaron family. Since they were all massacred with the exception of Edith, Kenneth, and me, Kenneth was the only one left to keep that secret hidden. When Kenneth disappeared the night his daughter was murdered by King Gene, many assumed he was murdered as well. Rather, Kenneth went into hiding and remained out of the public eye for years. It wasn't until the last five years when Shara took her post in The Port that Kenneth came out of hiding and began posing as a government official, which was easy to accomplish since many no longer recognized him and Shara was new to Allenthia. Currently, Kenneth serves as a direct advisor to her and smuggles out the weapons a little at a time.

In regard to the new bombs the Legion has been using

in recent attacks on the Royal Guard, these have been constructed in Anniah. If what Kenneth says is true, they have their own branch of the Legion, but they have access to abandoned underground laboratories just under the palace in Anniah. Kenneth was also privy to that information thanks to his other daughter, Edens. It is still strange to know my mother's name - Ellara. She seems fascinating in every way and I just wish I had the chance to get to know her.

As we speak, Kenneth's connections in Anniah are perfecting those bombs. They only detonate when they sense a minimum of five people around them. Their heat sources are the trigger, so when the bombs are deployed, they instantly search for heat signatures and explode when they sense that certain amount. Another unique ability they have is each bomb possesses a different characteristic. Some launch mini grenades and fireballs, while others shoot out hooks that drive into the ground and buildings and cause earthquakes.

Every detail hypes me up, until I think about Logan, Prince David, and Edith. What will my involvement in all of this do to them?

Kenneth thinks I should put some effort into participating in the chase for King David's hand in marriage, but I am completely torn on that. On one hand, I was thrilled for the opportunity to get to know the prince better just this morning. On the other hand, he has now become an obstacle. His grandfather murdered my family and now he possesses some reign over my nation. I am going to have to take it from him one way or another.

I drift off to sleep and do not wake until the princess slams the door to her room hours later. She must have enjoyed herself this evening.

We spend the next few days touring The Port and nearby cities of Allenthia. The placement of the Aaron palace is perfect. It is in the direct center of a ring of mountains and natural reservoirs that trickle off of the sides of those same mountains. This area is breathtaking.

I take mental pictures of the layout of The Port and where the most popular areas are. To me, these days of touring are more than just getting to know our surroundings. I appreciate every inch we cover and don't have to spend much effort convincing myself it is all worth fighting for. I do not know how or when I am going to take hold of my home, but I am anxiously waiting for that opportunity. I haven't heard from Kenneth since the night I found out who I really am, but this isn't a surprise. I am to wait until he has sufficient information to relay to me. Until then, I am to continue my role as a dedicated companion to Princess Lily, which is becoming increasingly harder these days.

Each day that we travel around the area and meet more citizens, Lily invites a new suitor to tour with us. They are not accustomed to having a companion in tow, so some of them send me on personal errands. What really irritates me is the fact that the princess allows it. In fact, she seems rather entertained by all of it. She is still punishing me for betraying her trust at the Royal Gala, and it makes my goal of overthrowing her and her family even more appealing.

I am on my way back to the palace from running one of those mindless errands for Lily and her suitor when Dell stops me at the entrance.

"Prince David has requested for you to return to the Golden Palace immediately. He said you would know what it concerns and would understand." Judging by the way she says this, I can tell David didn't reveal more information and she is absolutely flabbergasted. She is more accustomed to being in the loop on events that take place in Allenthia, but that will change when the Legion and I intervene. Teaming up with the Legion - that is something I hadn't processed until just now. I knew I would be working with Kenneth, but I didn't really think it through. This revelation excites me even more.

"Thank you, Dell. I will pack up my belongings and request a transport to the train." Packing doesn't take too long since I don't have much to pack to begin with. However, I do take my time to carefully pack my locket and the journal, which suddenly mean more to me than they did just a few days ago.

I arrive at the train station and am intercepted by Emma and her team. Apparently, there is no need for them to remain in The Port since I will not be here for them to style. When I inform Emma why I have been told to return to the Golden Palace, she takes this in stride and smiles for the first time since I met her. I am certain Kenneth has filled her in on the most recent developments, so she must understand that me becoming close to Prince David isn't just an opportunity for me to be successful, but for the Legion to be as well. Nevertheless, I still do not trust her. Princess Lily inadvertently told me Emma plays both sides, so I decide to tread lightly with her. I wait until the two of us are alone in a car and address my concern with her.

"I understand the Royal Adair family has successfully turned you into a paid informant. You have provided them with information on the Legion and I am honestly confused about where your alliances lay. If you are an opportunist and just trying to survive, I understand that, but trust me when I say that I do not trust you and will be watching you." Emma is chuckling. How does she find this entertaining? I am being completely serious and my anger is growing by the second. Meanwhile, she is laughing in my face.

"Elaine, settle down. Yes, I was paid for information I provided, but it wasn't accurate information. I told Prince David and Princess Lily-Beth the Legion was planning a strike in Anniah sometime in the next two weeks, which isn't factual in the slightest. I also told them the new weapons were generated in an underground lair in the Battle Grounds, which is another lie. The point was to convince them to direct their energy and forces towards Anniah and away from where the action is really beginning to develop. Kenneth asked me to move the heat off of The Port, the palace in Anniah, and the Battle Grounds so he can continue recruiting and strengthening those areas."

This makes sense when Emma explains it, but I am still hesitant to trust her. Emma must be able to read the look on my face and determine that I do not believe her.

"If you don't believe me, just ask Kenneth and Princess Lily-Beth about it." Emma knows I cannot reach Kenneth directly without her help, so that isn't an option. Lily, on the other hand, would be easy to ask, but who knows when I will see her again. She is to continue building relationships in Allenthia while I make an attempt to get to know the prince better.

"I appreciate you explaining the situation to me, but forgive me if I do not jump on the opportunity to instantly trust you on this one. How much has Kenneth told you about what I know?"

"Enough for me to know it would be unwise to cross you, especially if the plan you two are concocting actually works." I didn't think Kenneth would reveal so much to Emma yet, but I am glad he did. Maybe she and I could form a trusting bond after all.

We arrive in Aparthia and the first person I see is Logan. This should make for interesting dinner conversation.

Chapter 16

Logan takes my hand to guide me down the steps of the train and a knot builds in my stomach. I want to trust him so badly, but everything is so convoluted right now. The knot could be from nerves, but I think it is because I am anticipating a twist in the relationship we have built.

"How was the trip, Elly? Things have been quiet around here without you. Edith has been dying to see you."

"I've only been gone a week. I am sure you all have gone on just fine without me around to stir up trouble for everyone." I attempt to smile at Logan, but it doesn't come easily. Kenneth told me I shouldn't offer up all of the details I recently derived, but I don't think I can keep all of this in much longer.

"So, why the sudden push to bring you back? Prince David didn't tell me anything other than I had to send for your return right away." And the knot tightens... I don't know why it feels like a betrayal to tell Logan that I am supposed to participate in the pursuit of his younger brother, but it does.

"Apparently, I meet all of the expectations set forth by the Royal Adair family to take part in the social events surrounding Prince David in the coming weeks." The blood drains from Logan's face and he avoids making eye contact with me.

"Oh, I didn't realize you would be forced to take part in the competition for his royal hand." The sarcasm roles off of his tongue easily.

"I wasn't forced. Prince David asked me if I would like to participate before I left with the princess. I would be crazy not to give myself a chance to take a break from serving as a companion, right?" I partially mean what I am saying about it being an excuse to take a break, but I am mostly just trying to avoid hurting Logan's feelings. Up until the last week, we had built a relationship out of honesty and comfort with one another, so this conversation is a struggle for me to have.

"Of course. You're right. I completely understand." He doesn't, but he is trying to be kind. I can read it all over his face.

"How many desperate women that qualified actually showed up anyway?"

"Out of the thirty-six who initially met the guidelines, thirty were still unwed and out of those, two others rejected the invitation."

"So there are twenty-eight of us remaining? I wonder why the prince wanted me here now rather than later. I thought he would send for me later in the season."

"It must have something to do with King Rennin moving up the deadline for the marriage." The air just got a whole lot thinner.

"Why would he move up the date? When does he want the prince to get married?" Kenneth needs to know this immediately. This will move up the plans the Legion has set for their invasion. Their goal was to strike with a massive force the night of the wedding since Prince David and many members of the Royal Guard would be distracted. With the eyes of Aparthia on the wedding, other duties would be neglected, making the Legion's entrance easier.

"Initially, King Rennin selected April for the wedding,

but the prince was able to convince him to move the date to sometime in May."

"That means Prince David has two months to find a wife and get married. King Rennin drastically expedited this process. Any idea why?"

"You know, Elly? With all of the questions you are asking, you have me thinking you really want some time to get to know the prince." Bitterness is catching in his voice. I take a deep breath and try to relax just enough to build myself up again for the conversation that is to come between us.

We finally make it to my quarters and I have every intention of confronting Logan about who he is and why he didn't tell me directly, but then I notice Prince David waiting for me just inside the door. It is so strange to see the two brothers next to each other, even if one has no idea that they share more than just a role in the Royal Guard.

I curtsy and smile when our eyes catch. Logan takes one look at the two of us and departs quicker than I would have liked. The prince blushes just enough for me to notice and smiles with all of his teeth. They are perfectly straight and white. I hadn't noticed until just now.

"Hi, Elaine. How was the trip back? I'm sorry to

request your return so soon, but the situation has changed. My father adjusted the timeline to speed things up a bit."

"I don't mind at all. I was starting to miss the comfort of my own bed. Plus, Sue's food is way better."

"I have sent word to Emma and her team that they will need to get you ready for dinner this evening. I would like you to meet the ladies who will be staying with us for a while."

"Staying with us? Here? In the palace?"

"Yes, how else am I supposed to have enough time to get to know all of them? I would like as much time as possible with you all so I can give everyone an equal opportunity."

"Well, two months doesn't seem like enough time to get to know one person, let alone twenty-eight women." This unsettles Prince David and he excuses himself to get ready for dinner as well.

Emma and her team work quickly and by the time it is time for my departure to dinner, the butterflies in my stomach have already formed and the hair on my neck is standing. I enter the dining room and search the room for a familiar face. I cannot control my excitement when I see more than one familiar face, I see Edith, a girl who was second to me in rank at my school, Rebecca, and five others who were ranked in the top three in previous years at my school as well. Edith and I embrace and then I take a seat with Rebecca and the others.

It is comforting to know that I will be spending my days with eight young women who I am familiar with, aside from the fact that we are all essentially competition to one another. Six of us engage in conversation and giggle throughout dinner, while the other two watch us with scrutiny. Meanwhile, Prince David sits back and observes the show before him in silence. He talks to no one and appears to listen attentively to the conversations circulating the room. It isn't until our last course is served that he stands and addresses the room.

"Ladies, it is my pleasure to welcome you to the Golden Palace. As you all know, you are here so that I may get to know you better. You may also have heard that my father has the expectation that I will wed one of you within the next two months." The room swirls with excitement, but the prince continues anyway. "This is as exhilarating for me as it is all of you. However, this will not be a competition. You all will not compete against each other in any shape or form. Instead, I will spend time with each of you and will get to know you. If I feel like you are not the right fit for me, you will be paid in gold so that your time was not wasted and you will return to your homes." The abruptness of being told we could leave at any time silences the chatter in the room.

"Now, enjoy the rest of your meal. I will be meeting with a few of you at the conclusion of dinner." Prince David returns to his seat at the head of the table and Andrew begins making his rounds around the table to inform the women which ones will be spending the remainder of the evening with Prince David. I expect to receive an invitation when Andrew approaches me, but he passes right by me and invites Edith and Rebecca instead. He also invites two other women in the room, which means four women out of twenty-eight will be spending time with Prince David while I have to return to my room. This stings more than I would like it to, but I am not too ashamed. Prince David knows more about me than he does many of these other women in the room. I will have my time eventually. Plus, this might present me with another opportunity to talk to Logan.

I return to my room and there is no sign of Logan anywhere. I am disappointed, but not surprised. Since Princess Lily is not here, he does not have to tend to his post stationed in the hallway outside of her room. I take a long bath and put on my most comfortable satin pajamas. Tomorrow will be a busy day, I am sure, so I climb into bed and rest my eyes. I am almost asleep when I hear a girl crying outside of my room. I am betting she was asked to go home. Maybe this competition won't be so friendly after all.

The next morning, there are only twenty-six of us remaining at breakfast. Two were escorted out late last night. This makes me wonder what they did wrong for the prince to dismiss them so soon. If he decides I am not worth his time, will I be sent to serve elsewhere, or will I be allowed to continue in my trade as a companion to Princess Lily? If I want to carry out my plan to strike from within the Golden Palace, I have to find a way to stay here. This means I have to win over the prince or princess - either one will suffice at this point.

"What did you do last night? Did you get to spend time with the prince?" I ask Edith and Rebecca. Rebecca was just waiting to brag, so she dives in.

"It was wonderful. There is a private theater downstairs that the prince took us to. We watched old movies and ate so many delectable deserts. I've never had so much fun before. The best part was when the prince told the other two girls who were with us that they would be going home. They had no idea he was going to dismiss them so easily - none of us did. One burst into tears right then and there and the other just wanted her payment of gold before she left. What a night!"

"So it seems." I can't help but feel a pang of jealousy.

"No one cares about your frivolous evening. Do you really think any of you will peak the princes' interest? You are all so mundane and boring. Two of you are servants. It's revolting." One of the girls from my school says loud enough for everyone sitting around us to hear. The room grows silent. Rebecca is beside herself and bites her lip.

"Jael, is it? The fact that we are servants and the prince has asked us to be here anyway should make you feel threatened. He knows us and knows our trade, yet he invited us just as he invited you." I can tell by the way Jael's eyes narrow that she did not think I would have the audacity to speak to her. Her father is a high-ranking government official, so she must think she is more entitled than most here.

"And why would you be interesting to him? What will you have to talk about? The best way to scrub a floor?

The best detergent to use on his clothes? How utterly embarrassing!"

This time, it is Edith who speaks up first. "Actually, we discussed how many of the current government officials are getting too comfortable and fat in their positions. We both agreed that a cleansing of many of the government officials would be beneficial for the prince when he becomes king. That means your dear father might be out of a job soon. Then, I suppose you will be the one learning how to scrub floors. Shall I teach you now so you are better prepared for what is to come?" This just burns Jael. She is about to explode when the prince walks in and everyone rises just in time to curtsy.

"There is no need for any of that from here on out. Otherwise, we will spend more time with formalities rather than talking about important matters. Isn't that right, Ms. Edith?" Based on the tone in his voice, I gather he heard the conversation and did not appreciate Edith divulging his conversation with others. It won't be long and Edith will be asked to leave, which might not be such a bad thing for her considering she is the princess of Anniah - not that I have had time to tell her yet. Kenneth's plan is for me to fill her in just before the Legion attacks. That way, we have time to recruit her and insert her into her rightful place as queen over Anniah once Aparthia has been dominated.

"Today, a few of you will be spending time with me in the courtyard. The rest of you may do as you please. You may enjoy our many amenities, such as the library, theater, or gym. You may also relax in your rooms or tour the rest of the palace if you would like to do so. Please finish breakfast and you will be notified if you are to spend time with me this afternoon." Just like that, he makes a grand entrance and then leaves. We spend the rest of breakfast gorging ourselves and then disperse to our rooms in anticipation of receiving an invitation to this afternoon's festivities with Prince David.

Chapter 17

I am absolutely thrilled when there is a knock at my door. I am not expecting company, so that must mean I am receiving an invitation to this afternoon's events with David. I know I should be distancing myself emotionally from the prince, but the excitement building is too much for me to ignore. I open the door and I am not disappointed. Andrew smiles as he hands me an invitation. I am opening it before the door closes behind me, leaving Andrew in the hallway.

"Prince David requests for you to join him in the courtyard in approximately one hour. Wear something comfortable to participate in the games that are afoot." If I'm being honest with myself, all of this is a game;

however, I suspect he means a physical competition of some sort. This should be invigorating, considering many of the women present do not look as though physical challenges are enticing to them.

I rummage through my drawers to find an appropriate outfit and land on the perfect one. I change into black tights that end just beneath my calves and a fitted black tank top with mesh sides. Fitted clothing isn't usually my first pick, but I think it is appropriate for the task at hand. I then retrieve two golden ribbons that usually hold my curtains back. They glitter when they catch the sunlight just right, so I think they will serve their purpose well. I then divide my hair into two tight braids and weave a gold ribbon through each braid. Against my dark brown hair, the gold looks even more striking than I anticipated. I lace up my running shoes and head for the door. Just before I reach for the golden knob, I decide it would be best to remove my locket from around my neck and secure it in Logan's journal back on the bookshelf.

In an effort not to seem overly anxious, I take my time as I wind my way through the hallways and reach the courtyard. Evidently, I was not the only anxious lady because there are already others spread out around the courtyard when I arrive. As I look around and count heads, there are thirteen of us total, which is exactly half of the remaining group. The only face I recognize is Jael. There is no sign of Edith or Rebecca, which is disheartening.

"Ladies, thank you for joining me this afternoon. As you may have already noticed, there are thirteen of you present, fourteen including me. I realize that is quite a large group, but for what I have planned, I needed enough to make two teams. If you look in the center of the court before you, you will see three golden hoops, one on top of the other. The object of the game is to pass the ball back and forth between teammates and throw it into the hoops. The hard part will be tossing the ball perfectly so that it goes through all three hoops. If your throw is slanted in any way, the ball will likely only pass through the first hoop and then bounce off the second. The ball is not to touch the ground at any point. If it does, the defending team will take possession of the ball. The first team to reach three points wins. Any questions?" The prince looks around the courtyard and studies the faces of the women gaping at him.

"Are there any rules concerning touching or fouling opposing team members?" one of the girls asks.

The prince grins when he responds. "Just don't get too

rough. We wouldn't want any of you to be too banged up for the rest of the week's festivities I have planned for you."

Many of the women look around at the faces next to them, some out of fear and others out of restlessness. I stare on at the prince and meet his grin. This should be fun indeed.

Prince David divides us into teams purely by appearance. It is evident he is trying to generate two equally powerful teams based on height, strength, and weight. He knows what I am capable of, but I wonder how this will work out for the other women. No one requests to be left out of the game, so that is a pleasant surprise. When the prince reaches the last two girls, he sends them to their appropriate sides and announces that he will be on the opposing team from me, along with Jael, who is glaring at me with such intensity at the moment. Andrew then provides each team with colored bands to differentiate between the two. My team has blue and Prince David's team is given red.

We have two minutes to speak among our teammates before the game begins so we huddle up and strive to come up with a plan for triumph. At first, everyone seems too timid to lead, so I intervene and offer up a plan of defense. I pair up everyone with someone of equal size on the opposing team and am just about to discuss offense when the prince announces we have twenty seconds until we start.

"Just give the ball to me" is all I have time to spit out.

"Ding!" The ball is tossed up into the air and David reaches for it and tucks it under his arm. As he runs towards the hoop, everyone seems too afraid to move.

"Get the ball!" I yell as loud as I can. My team springs into action and suddenly everyone begins moving their feet. I am about to block the prince when I am side checked and thrown off my feet. When I look up, Jael is staring at me with a smug smile on her face. Now I know this is more than just a game to her. I am her competition and she has every intention of putting me in the place she thinks I belong. The prince easily tosses the ball in the first hoop, and it makes its way through the second and third glistening hoops. That's one point for the prince's team.

"Ding!" The ball is tossed up for a second time, and this time, I position myself to jump up and tip the ball so one of the girls from my team is able to grasp it. She catches it and quickly hands it off to another girl, who then attempts to make her way to the hoop. She makes it about two steps before a girl from David's team, Paige, trips her and catches the ball as it is thrown into the air. She throws the ball into the first hoop, but it bounces off of the second. A girl from my team rebounds and catches the ball. She shoots and makes it through all three hoops easily, which is in large part because the girl is so tall. She towers over most of us, so scoring isn't too difficult for her. The score is now tied with one point each.

We go back and forth for a while and eventually tie again at two points each. At this point, everyone is tired and a water break is called for. When we break, we sit with our teammates and try to recuperate. Many of my own teammates have taken devastating blows from Jael. She is feisty and no one has the courage to pair up against her again. Ultimately, I end up securing the position against Jael. This is my chance to get her back for side checking me earlier in the game. I will not let her get the best of me.

As I look at the other team to see if they appear to be as disheveled as my team, I catch Prince David staring at me. He smiles and nods at me. I return the gesture and feel my cheeks begin to blossom. Knowing the prince has an eye on me makes my stomach ache, but in a good way.

"Ding!" The final play has begun and the animosity is growing by the second. Everyone wants to impress the prince so the teams have disappeared and everyone is out for their own now. I don't blame any of the girls for this, but the chaos of everyone trying to showoff is a bit much. The ball is dropped and thrown out so many times that this last play is the longer than the first few combined. When the ball is tossed up again, I reach for it and shove Jael out of the way as I jump into the air. I quickly tuck the ball, but not before Jael throws a wicked left elbow into my sensitive nose. My entire face is throbbing and I can see blood, but I pivot my right foot and turn away from Jael. Everyone is on me before I can take another step. I try to turn back, but Jael is still hot on my right. The only option is to discard the ball. I look up and act like I am looking for a teammate and then toss the ball up. Everyone reacts and thinks I am throwing the ball in the direction I was looking. Instead, I just catch the ball again and run through the newly formed gap to the hoop. Jael doesn't give up easily and neither does Prince David. I am between the two and can't spot an exit. When I turn and face Jael, she clutches her right fist and I can tell she means to plant another hit on me. I duck and she strikes Prince David in the face instead. Out of pure disbelief, she freezes and I seize the moment. I push off of her thigh to create more thrust as I jump toward the hoop. I am shocked when it makes it through all three hoops and turn to the rest of my team for approval and cheers. Instead, I see a crowd forming around the prince who is now lying on the ground. Jael must have punched him harder than I thought. I shove my way through the tight circle and am relieved when I see the prince chuckling on the ground.

"I am so incredibly sorry, Prince David. I did not mean to punch you. I was trying to..." Jael has made a fool of herself and I am loving every second of it.

"Trying to hit Elaine, I know. Don't worry about it. It is all part of the game." The prince is taking this in stride, but he now has a bloody nose that matches mine. When he attempts to smile again, he gently touches the tip of his nose and grimaces. Andrew helps him up and offers him a towel.

"Please, give the towel to Elaine. She looks worse than me. Besides, if I am not mistaken, she scored the winning point." Everyone seems to have forgotten about the game. We are all still in astonishment over the fact that Jael just punched the prince in the nose. Nonetheless, we did win and I did score the final point. This, combined with Jael's bad luck, makes me feel pretty good.

"Thank you, Prince David, but I have grown accustomed to the pain over the last few weeks." I try to joke.

Everyone is dismissed, with the exception of David and me. We stay back for the Golden Palace's private doctor to tend to us. We are quite the pair next to each other. We are both holding bloody towels up to our faces and waiting for the doctor to fix us up.

"What a game! I really didn't think some of those girls had it in them. I suppose I should have figured their fangs would come out when I pinned them against one another, though," the prince admits.

"You never can read a person until you throw him or her into a competition, especially one as important as this one."

"What do you mean by important, per say?" David questions.

"Well, we all wanted to impress you, so we forgot about the whole team aspect and just did what we could to catch your attention. The chaos caused is insurmountable, wouldn't you say?"

"So you do want to impress me?"

I wasn't prepared for that. I gulp and stutter when I respond. "I was speaking on behalf of the other women, not necessarily myself. I just don't like to lose." I smile when

I say this, so hopefully David knows I'm only half lying.

When the doctor finishes examining us, he prescribes more of the wonderful medicine Princess Lily provided me with before and we return to our rooms to prepare for dinner.

I rush to my room, eager for a warm bath, only to find my door isn't closed properly after close inspection. When I enter, Logan is perched on my bed and holding not only his journal, but my locket as well. My breath catches and I shove through the door. I suppose this conversation cannot wait.

Chapter 18

"When were you going to tell me you read my journal?"

"When were you going to tell me who you really are, Thomas?" I can tell the use of his real name surprises him.

"I suppose it would have been about the same time as when you told me who you really are, Princess Elaine." That one stings.

"Well, where do we go from here? We have obviously been hiding so much from each other, so I don't think there is any point in holding anything back now, do you?" I ask harsher than I intended. "Just tell me why you left that journal in here to begin with. Did you mean for me to find it?"

Logan takes a deep breath and appears to think before

he speaks. "Of course I wanted you to find it. I just didn't know if you had yet. I wanted to see if it had even been touched, but then I found your locket inside and knew you read it."

"If you knew who the people in the pictures of the locket were that night Edith and I opened it, why didn't you say anything then?"

"I wasn't sure if you were ready for that burden of information yet. I knew who you and Edith were the first night you two arrived here. Kenneth told me to expect you and keep an eye on you. I knew the best way I could keep up with you was to put a bug in Princess Lily's ear that Judith had been slacking the last few weeks. I did this just before you two entered the room of the choosing ceremony, which ensured she wouldn't be able to choose any of the previous people presented. Once I mentioned it, she took the bait and ran with it. At that point, I knew either you or Edith would end up in this room. Either way, one of you would be assigned this room and find my journal.

"Why couldn't you just tell me who you were instead of waiting until I read it in a random book placed nonchalantly in my room?"

"What was I supposed to say? Hi, my name is Thomas,

but I go by Logan because I am the long lost Adair prince that disappeared seventeen years ago."

This does sound silly when he says it like that, but it would have made things a lot easier.

"None of this explains why you are still posing as an officer in the Royal Guard and communicating with Kenneth when you could be sitting on a throne." This part seems harder for Logan to explain. He composes himself and pauses before he responds.

"When I found out who I really was a few years ago, I made my way into Aparthia and paid to meet King Rennin. I told him who I was, with the expectation of being welcomed back with open arms. Instead, King Rennin told me something I never anticipated. He claimed that my mother got pregnant with me out of wedlock before the two of them were married. As a result, King Gene and Queen Majorie's father, who was a prominent government official during that time, arranged the marriage between King Rennin and Queen Majorie. In doing so, this quickly secured a wife for King Rennin in case King Gene died at an early age and kept Queen Majorie from the disgrace of raising a son without a father and out of wedlock. Luckily, I was not born until about seven and a half months after the royal wedding, so they just told everyone I was born prematurely."

"So, you aren't really King Rennin's firstborn and no one ever knew of Queen Majorie's pregnancy before they were married?"

"Right. I was a complete scandal. However, when Kenneth conveniently stole me from my mother when I was three years old, King Rennin no longer had to worry about me securing the throne instead of a true heir of his. He never sent out a search party and just told everyone I died of medical complications. He also paid everyone off who knew anything about the kidnapping so there would be no further discussions of such."

I am trying to process all of this, but it is hard to keep up with all of the twists Logan is throwing at me right now.

"King Rennin was glad when I was gone, so he was completely aghast when I returned and hoped to be a part of his family again. There was no way he was going to give me the chance to reclaim my place as the first Adair son, so he dismissed me and paid me in gold to disappear quietly."

"What did you do? How did you end up back here?"

"I took the gold and went back to Kenneth. I didn't have anywhere to go. Besides, Kenneth raised me like his own for so many years, so I did feel like I belonged with him. Things have never been like they were before, but we now have a common goal to achieve. You see, ever since I saw the real King Rennin when he flicked me off like a bug on his shoulder, I knew he was no longer fit to be a leader. So many secrets and incidents of betrayal, how could I trust him to lead Aparthia? Knowing Kenneth had other plans in mind, I agreed to contribute and join the Legion. So, I saved the gold King Rennin gave me and waited until I was old enough to draft into the Royal Guard. After years of training with the Legion, I was no longer scrawny and looked more rugged and suntanned than I did before. All I had to do at that point to make myself disguisable was cut and dye my hair slightly darker than it was naturally. Over time, I worked my way up the ranks and now, here we are. King Rennin has never taken a second look at me."

"But why would you choose to come here out of all places? What if he did suddenly recognize you one day?"

"Kenneth knew it was only a matter of time before King Rennin began questioning when the Aaron and Ackert princesses would show their faces, especially because Kenneth is the one who started the whispers of such, and figured he would begin to make changes to control the situation, starting with the choosing ceremony. He watched both you and Edith and knew the you would end up in the Golden Palace when you did - hence, the importance of my role here. I have been keeping track of what goes on in the Royal Guard briefings and communicating with Kenneth when I need to. It was also my duty to inform you of who I am and who you are. That was a difficult task, though, and I tried to be a nudging hand along the way. Besides, with the cameras around, I never felt safe enough to discuss details of such importance. Now that we both know who we really are, it is time to figure out what we want to do with this information."

It makes sense, but I still don't quite understand why Logan just didn't tell the nation who he is and put up a fight against King Rennin. What about his mother in all of this? Then again, the king would probably have arranged for Logan to be killed if he caused a stir of any kind.

"What about your mother? I'm certain she has been holding out hope for all of these years that you would return to her one day."

"That is another reason I fought so hard to make my way into the Golden Palace. I wanted to be around my mother and get to know her without causing too big of a rift. The little I have been around her has made it worth it to me. One day, when the time is right, I will explain all of this to her. Until then, I am going to keep my distance, but still be in the presence of my real mother, who has been innocent in all of this. As for my brother and sister, I have been forming bonds with them as well and gaining their trust, so when all of this is over, we might be able to hang on to some aspect of our relationships and become a family. Conversely, I have also become a member of David's inner circle, which has provided me with some very valuable information. That might be a line in the sand in David's eyes."

"Now, Elaine, where do you go from here?"

Wow. For the first time in my life, I am utterly dumbfounded. I am sitting in the presence of a prince who does not want to be a prince and I am now about to discuss a plan to overthrow his family and right to the throne. This is a conundrum if I ever heard one.

Chapter 19

At breakfast the next morning, there are now only fifteen of us remaining. Eleven were let go within the last twenty-four hours, some right after our game ended and some during dinner last night. My guess is the prince was able to tell some of the women who participated in the game were not competitive and tough enough for his liking. As for the others, they hadn't quite caught his attention yet during the short time they were here. If you don't intrigue him, you are gone - lesson learned. I am pleased that Edith and Rebecca are still here, but astounded as to why Jael is still here. She did punch the prince in the face yesterday. Doesn't that merit a ticket home?

As I look across the table at Edith, I am still torn as to whether or not I should fill her in on everything Logan and I discussed. We decided it would be best to leave her out of everything for now out of fear of putting her and the Legion at risk, but as we grow closer, the pit in my stomach strengthens. I know I am willing to risk everything and fight as a part of the Legion when the time is right, but I don't think Edith could do the same. She came from a loving home and had a relatively normal childhood, unlike me, which is why I'm not in a hurry to take all of that away from her just yet. We will fill her in when it is necessary.

The goal remains the same for me. I am to do what I can to draw closer to the prince and gain his trust. If any pertinent information arises, I report it to either Logan or Emma so they can reach Kenneth. I still don't really trust Emma, though, so Logan will be my first choice.

Logan advised me to remain professional with David and discard any feelings I have for him, but that will be a difficult task, just like it has been tough to ignore my feelings for Logan. When I think about it, I genuinely care for both of them, but they are brothers and whether I like it or not, they have each kept secrets from me. All I can do at this point is remain impartial with both men and remain on the trek to do what it takes to take back my nation from the Adair family's grasp. Ironically, I'm in the running to marry into that same family. Tricky situation.

In the next few days, Prince David takes more time to get to know the few of us remaining and our numbers begin to dwindle a little at a time. We are now down to eight women, including Edith, Rebecca, Jael, and myself. I have gotten to know the other four girls, Paige, Stassi, Genesis, and Ashton, and I am becoming friends with them as well.

I didn't think it would be possible, but they have grown on me so much so that when our numbers decrease even more, it will be hard to part ways, with the exception of Jael, of course. She is free to leave at any time, but I doubt that will happen soon enough. She is determined to win Prince David's hand in marriage. She has even gone to the extent of trying to sabotage the rest of us. When poor Rebecca was engaging in a conversation with David, Jael bumped into her, causing her red drink to spill all over her elegant yellow gown. Then, she somehow managed to slip when she was carrying sharp scissors and *accidentally* cut Stassi's gorgeously long hair. Stassi had to cut off about six inches, which actually highlights all of her facial features and makes her even more devilishly attractive. That one worked in Stassi's favor, but others haven't been so lucky. Jael hasn't messed with Edith, Rebecca, or me too much yet. She must know the three of us will introduce her to a wrath like this nation has never witnessed before if she tries anything that petty with us.

Breakfast concludes and we disband to enjoy a variety of amenities. Paige, Edith, Rebecca, and I are on our way to the theater to watch a movie when we feel the walls of the palace rumble just enough for us to reach for the walls to steady ourselves. We are silent, but continue on to the theater. Sometimes, the Royal Guard participates in drills, so this isn't the first time something like this has happened. We take a few steps and then continue our discussion, but stop short when a stampede of Royal Guard members rush down our hallway and practically throw us out of the way. That is odd, but none of the warning alarms have gone off. Just another drill.

"Attention Golden Palace personnel! Make your way to your rooms immediately. This is not a drill." Now the alarms are sounding.

The four of us clutch hands and make our way towards my room, since it is the closest to our current location. When we are just feet away from my door, the lights go out and we are standing in complete darkness. I can't even see the hand I am holding anymore. Another rush of feet pummels through us and we are sent flying to the sides. I crawl on the floor until I reach a hand and begin guiding the girl to my door. When we get there, the door is swung open and I am pulled in.

The individual who is holding my wrist also holds a flashlight in his other hand. I am relieved when I recognize the face as David's.

I stammer out the questions before he can even speak. "What's going on? What are you doing here? Are you alright?" Then, as quick as I was pulled in, I am yanked into his chest. David is hugging me. His heart is thumping and he is breathing heavily.

"The Golden Palace is under attack. They haven't breached the gates yet, but they are giving it their best effort. We barely had a warning they were coming, but I just had enough time to get my parents to safety and give the Royal Guard their orders. Then, I had to make sure you were safe. I rushed down here to your room, and when you weren't here, I panicked." I wait for him to continue, but he finally turned his flashlight and landed on the fact that there are other girls with me. He instantly drops his arms from around me and stiffens.

He clears his throat and continues. "I was worried

about all of you. Thank goodness you three are okay."

Three? There were four of us two minutes ago. I feverishly look around and see that Edith is missing.

"You have to find Edith! She was just with us!"

"I will, but first, I need to escort you three to a holding room."

Almost like they were listening the entire time, members of the Royal Guard swarm us and begin jogging us down the hallways, down several stair cases, and through a multitude of rooms, some of which I've never seen before. Meanwhile, so many questions are forming in my head. Why is the Legion attacking now? Is it even the Legion? Where is Kenneth? Is Logan okay? Where did Edith go?

The more I think of these things, the more nauseous I become. Thankfully, we reach what I assume is the holding room and are practically shoved in. When I look around the room, I see other familiar faces. Sue is here and she is holding, of all people, Jael who is shuddering and crying hysterically. I also see Emma huddled in the corner with most of her styling team and Ashton. Still no sign of Genesis or Edith.

I can't hold it in any longer. I reach for the nearest trashcan and see my breakfast again for a second time.

This is not how I envisioned myself responding when the planned attack did occur. This one is completely unexpected. I feel a gentle hand on my back and expect to see Rebecca or Paige, but when I feel the rough callouses graze my neck, I know it is David. I wipe my mouth and turn to face him, full of embarrassment.

His eyes look concerned and sincere. "Don't worry - everything will be okay. It will end soon. We were taken by surprise, but that surprise has now been replaced with anger and years of training. We will push them back and things will be back to normal shortly. I have to get out there, but I need to know you are going to stay here and look out for everyone in here while I am gone. You cannot leave until I come and get you."

I don't know why I agree so easily, but I nod my head and stare deep into his large golden eyes. I want to hug him and tell him to come back as fast as he can, but I remember that this attack could be because of me. I must stay strong. I clench his hand and tell him to be careful. He pivots on his heels and dashes away before I can even place my hand back by my side. I look around the dark room and am thankful when it seems no one was paying attention to our brief interaction. All I can do now is wait.

Chapter 20

After spending the night in the safe room, the door finally opens and we see light for the first time in hours. Many fell asleep, but I couldn't even attempt to close my eyes. I am too scared of everything going on around me, this attack I know nothing about, where Logan and I stand, the building connection between David and me, the Legion, where Edith is… Every time I closed my eyes, a new fear would flash before me.

A Royal Guardsman begins ushering everyone out of the room. "Everyone, please return to your posts and rooms. The attack is over. We are safe now." I know I should be relieved, but I don't think I will be until I see David and Logan.

"Is there any word on where the other girls are? Are they alright?"

"We are not completely certain at the moment. We know Miss Genesis decided to return back to her family this morning after the commotion of last night, but we still have not found Miss Edith. Guards are looking for her as we speak." I sink to my knees and begin to cry. Suddenly, I am completely overwhelmed by everything that has happened in recent days. Edith missing just sent me over the edge.

Rebecca crouches down and wraps her arms around me in an effort to calm me. "Don't worry, they will find her. Edith is tougher than any of us. She can take care of herself." As she says this, I realize why Edith's disappearance is truly bothering me. She is the only real family I have left in this world. Yes, it's all a very strange chain of events, but we are family and we are all each other has, whether we both realize it or not.

"Elaine! What happened? What's going on?" Logan arrives just in time. When I can't find the energy to pick myself up off of the floor, he scoops me up into his robust arms and carries me to my room, Rebecca and Paige in tow. I know they are trying to help, but all I want is to be alone right now. I am exhausted and don't have an ounce of energy remaining to entertain guests in my room at the moment. One look into Logan's blue eyes and he seems to read my thoughts.

"Ladies, I am sure Elaine just needs rest. Please use this time to contact your families and let them know you are safe. Then, get some rest yourselves. Dinner is planned for this evening, so you may reconvene then." I offer a small smile as the two depart. Then, I can't help but rest my head on Logan's chest. This feels safe and like home, something I've never experienced before.

Logan easily strides to my bed and sets me down softly. We stay like that for a few minutes - me sitting quietly on the bed, staring off into nothing, and Logan looking down at me out of concern.

"I was worried about you. Why did Kenneth strike earlier than planned? He put all of us at risk."

"Based on the information we have been able to gather, it wasn't Kenneth and the Legion who attacked us. In fact, we are still trying to piece all of it together."

"Tell me what's going on. Maybe I can help."

"I don't know if you are up for it right now. Maybe you should rest now and I'll fill you in later." This infuriates me. I understand that I just had a weak moment, but that doesn't give Logan another reason to hide more secrets from me until he thinks I am strong enough. Logan must read the emotions on my face because he begins to stammer on.

"Well, when we couldn't find any trace of Edith or Andrew, we went back and looked at the footage on the hall cameras. The explosions interrupted much of it, but we did have spurts where we were able to identify their locations. Just before the first bomb was detonated, Edith almost looked like she knew it was coming. It was the strangest thing. You all were walking down the main hall towards the theater when she trailed off behind you. Then, she looked right up at the camera and paused, as if she knew we would be watching her. That's when the first bomb hit and the lights went out. By the time you and the other girls made it to your room, she was gone. The next time we were able to identify her on usable footage, we caught a glimpse of her running across the front lawn, towards the gates."

"That doesn't make sense at all. Why would she run towards the attackers instead of away from them? There has to be a viable explanation for all of this."

"She certainly knew something was going to happen. Why else would she pause and look directly into the camera?"

"Maybe that was the first time she noticed it and found it intriguing."

"That's possible, but it still doesn't explain why she was running toward the source of heat during the attack."

I try to take this in stride, but none of it adds up. "What about Andrew? Were you able to see him in any of the footage?"

"The details of Andrew are even more perplexing. When we isolated the frames of him, we found him in the library just before chaos broke loose."

"What's strange about that? David sends him there frequently when he isn't in need of his service."

"It isn't the fact that he was in the library, but rather what he was doing in the library. When we zoomed in on him, we could see him tearing out maps of the layout of the Golden Palace and Aparthia out of books and stashing them in the folds of his uniform. Why would he need information like that? What use could he have for them?"

"Are those maps not common knowledge?"

"Many of them are, but he took them out of an official Golden Palace manual, which means those are extensively more detailed than the ones released to the public."

I shudder when I think about what could happen if

those maps fell into the wrong hands, unless Andrew is that set of wrong hands. What have Edith and Andrew gotten themselves into?

"Was there any trace of Andrew after that?"

"We were unable to pick up anymore captures of him, so we are thinking he utilized the underground tunnels that are hidden under the Golden Palace. They have been abandoned for years, so none of us thought they were usable. Andrew must have discovered them in those maps. They lead to an area just before the Battle Grounds, so we sent Royal Guardsmen there to scour the area for Andrew."

"What will happen to Edith or Andrew if they are found?"

"In the Adair family's eyes, they are traitors. If they are captured, they will be put to death."

This can't be. I just found out I have a living family member and now she is going to be taken from me, too. When my eyes don't meet Logan's, I sense he is just now processing why all of this is so hard for me. He pulls me up and embraces me.

"Don't worry, Elly. We will figure all of this out. I am sure Edith has a justifiable rationalization as to why she left. Maybe she was fleeing out of fear. We won't know until we find her. I promise you that I will search for her myself."

I don't know why this comforts me so much, but it does. Without thinking about it, I reach up and pull his face down to mine. I kiss him and panic when he doesn't kiss me back. Right when I try to free myself of his masculine arms, he pulls me closer and kisses me with such force that I almost fall backwards.

At dinner that evening, we come to the stark reality that despite the intimidating recent events that unfolded, we are still here to pursue Prince David. There are now six of us remaining since Genesis and Edith departed on their own will. Prince David enters with Logan at his side and I can't bring myself to look at either one of them.

We all wait for the prince to offer some sort of enlightenment on the events of the last twenty-four hours when he finally addresses us.

"Ladies, as you all know, we were attacked by a group who we have yet to identify at this point. Whoever they were, their numbers and weapons were not great enough to breach our gates. Yes, they invoked fear into many, but they did not beat us. Casualties were minimal and we are confident they will not return again for quite some time, if ever. That being said, you have the freedom to choose whether or not you would like to continue on this journey with me. If you would like to return home, you will receive a plentiful amount of gold for you and your family, as well as a private transport there as soon as you would like. However, if you elect to stay, with numbers as few as we now have, I would very much like to spend time with each of you individually to ensure I make the best decision when this is all over."

I know I kissed Logan just hours ago, but I am still pulled to David as well. I admire both of them for their diverse characteristics and am drawn in different directions toward both of them.

I look around the dinner table at the five other women present, Rebecca, Paige, Jael, Ashton, and Stassi. I am starting to think we are all in this for the long haul, when Stassi admits that she would like to return home.

...And then there were five of us.

Chapter 21

The days draw on and things are beginning to settle down. I am beginning to think the Legion has abandoned their plans to take back Allenthia from King Rennin's hold in the near future now that another group has evolved, until I receive a message from Kenneth. Through Emma, he sent a letter specifying that now that Logan has updated him on the most recent events surrounding the attack, Kenneth would like to move up the Legion's date of strike to avoid conflicting with timelines of the unknown group. He wants to seize control over the Adair family before someone else has the opportunity to do so. As a result, his instructions for me consist of continuing my pursuit of David and planting a bug in his ear. He didn't have to instruct me to continue on my quest for him because that is something I am already doing on my own. I desire to not only help the Legion, but myself also. Yes, strong feelings are developing for David, so there's that aspect, but I am also striving to keep the bigger picture in mind. If I am to release Allenthia from King Rennin's grip, I need to be able to identify the weaknesses of this nation's leading figures and structure. I think I can do that as long as I gain the trust of David and possibly get him to do what is best for Aparthia rather than his father.

I am going over and over the details of Kenneth's letter when someone knocks on the door to the library where I have spent much of my time recently. It is quiet, but as Andrew demonstrated, provides a wealth of information to wandering eyes as well.

I place the letter in my pocket and cross the room to the door. Before I can turn the handle, a figure is emerging from the doorway. I cannot make out who it is just yet because the face is completely covered by a breathtaking array of flowers. I cover my mouth with my hand as an attempt to hide the silly grin I must be sporting at the moment and then step around the circumference of the flowers to see who is carrying them. I am pleasantly surprised when I see it is David.

"Well, that is quite an entrance, I must say."

David smiles and responds so easily that I almost miss the hint of nervousness in his voice. "It had to be if I wanted to catch your attention."

"You have had it for quite some time now. No need for extravagant gestures anymore. However, if these are for me, I am not complaining."

"May I escort you to your room so we can put them on display in there?"

We walk towards my room and pass a few of the girls on the way. I can see steam blowing out of Jael's ears when we pass her. Rebecca, on the other hand, is silently cheering me on. At this point, we are all on the same page in that we just don't want the prince to select Jael over the rest of us. I haven't quite been able to wrap my head around why she is even here at this point. He must see her devilish ways, so there has to be a greater reason as to why he hasn't sent her packing.

David finds a suitable table for my flowers and sets them down. "When you have time, make sure you scrutinize those flowers. You might find something hidden in them."

I love surprises, so now I am sitting on the edge of my seat dying to tear the beautiful arrangement apart.

"Thank you for the flowers. They are stunning and if I am not mistaken, it is a combination of a variety of lilies, right?"

"It is. I know how much you enjoy your time spent in the courtyard, so I thought you might appreciate a little piece of it in here."

"Speaking of lilies, have you heard from your sister? I haven't heard a thing about her since my departure weeks ago. Has she found the man of her dreams yet?"

"I haven't talked to her much myself, but my parents say she is fairing well. She misses home and is ready to return, but my father is adamant she continues her journey in Allenthia. She is to travel to Anniah this afternoon with a gentleman by her side that she seems to favor."

"She actually found someone? That is shocking. I figured she would avoid fraternizing at all costs."

"Apparently, this one is quite the gentleman. She might get married one day after all. Now, the reason I am here is to ask if you would be willing to go on a date with me this evening - just the two of us? As you might already know, I have been spending time with the other women and you are the only one I have yet to make time for."

"I did notice, but I wasn't worried. I figured you were

saving the best for last." That lie came easily enough. The truth is I have been extremely jealous, but with everything else going on, I was able to push those feelings aside for the time being. "That being said, I would love to go on a date with you."

"There is something else. I wanted to do - something with your permission." This has me intrigued and a bit edgy. "Would it be alright if I kissed you?" I can feel my blush spreading to my ears. My whole face is on fire.

"I suppose that would be acceptable." In an effort to ease the tension, I close my eyes and lean in. The prince cups my face ever so gently and kisses me. It is soft and sweet, so different from my kiss with Logan, but still just as enjoyable. Before he pulls away, I catch a smile spreading across my face. When I open my eyes, his eyes are still closed and his facial expression tells me he has been waiting a while to do that.

"That was…"

"Perfect," I finish for him.

"Indeed. It was perfect. Now, I better be off. I have a plethora of meetings to attend before our date this evening." He gently gives me a quick peck on the nose and then departs.

Before I hear the door latch closed, I am on my feet and springing for the flowers. I jostle them around a bit until I see them. There are notes pinned to the stems of each flower. I tear the first one off and begin reading.

"I like the way your smile almost touches your eyes when you are really happy." I reach for another. "I like the way your eyes light up when you see me." Another. "I like your pointed nose." I read all twelve notes, each one as adorable as the previous. David wrote out twelve reasons he likes me.

I suddenly have the urge to kiss the prince again and cannot wait. I bolt for the door and practically sprint down the hall, dodging Royal Guardsmen as I pass. Then, I hear David's voice and halt. I glance into the doorway of the room his voice is coming from. This is strange. This room belongs to Jael. I shove the door open just a crack more and see the two standing there with their arms wrapped around each other. I close my eyes and try to shake off the image I just saw. When I open them, I see David kissing Jael. My chest is burning with anger. I spin around and head back to my room, stomping my feet with such force that I draw the attention of the same guards I just shoved my way by just seconds ago.

You win, Kenneth. The relationship between Prince David and me is now purely professional. If David wants to play games, I can be better at them.

I am halfway down the hall when there is a roar of an eruption. My feet come out from under me and I scramble to catch myself on the satin of the nearest wall. The lights are still on, but it is still hard to see. Everything is shaking and rumbling. As quickly as it commenced, the roaring stops.

A hoard of Royal Guard pushes their way through me. I spin around and follow them, assuming they are heading towards wherever the explosion occurred. I want to see what happened for myself since I obviously cannot take the word of David to be true any longer. We arrive in the main room of the Golden Palace and I almost slam into one of the men I was following. Why has everyone stopped so abruptly? I squeeze through the group and suddenly halt just as quickly as the guards did, mouth open and fists tightening.

"What are you doing here? How did you get back in?"

"I came to reclaim what is rightfully mine, something your father took from me years ago. Speaking of which, you might want to send a few men to check on him in his quarters. Things might be a little messy in there."

Prince David does what is suggested and sends a few guards to King Rennin's bedroom.

"What do you want?" David persists.

"I am Princess Edith Ackert of Anniah and I am here to seize control of my nation." I am stunned. The entire room is silent. Edith has known who she is all along. She even had the foresight to plan an escape and then an attack when we least expected it. This is not the same girl I came to know and think of as family. She spots me in the crowd and winks at me.

"Yes, Elaine, I know who I am. I have known since I was just a girl. Kenneth left me with family, but they were not keen on his plan to keep them quiet and me in the dark until he was ready. I have also known who you are. Do you think it was a coincidence that we ended up in the same room that first night? Was it also just a coincidence that I let you see the key to your locket? It has all worked just as I planned it would."

"If you knew, why didn't you tell me? I might have helped you." My voice is small compared to this dashingly strong woman in front of me, but I have to ask.

"Because Grandpa Kenneth obviously had other plans in mind for you. You have been his chosen one from the start of all of this. I didn't want to wait. I am taking my chances and carrying this out with or without you." I am just another citizen of Aparthia to her, not the family we were meant to be. This stings and I take it in without speaking another word. The time will come when we will see each other again and it won't be in the presence of so many onlookers. I certainly will not bite my tongue then.

"Now, as I was saying, I will be taking Anniah out of your control immediately. You are to remove all Royal Guard representatives and Aparthia government officials from Anniah immediately. If you do not get them out of there, I will give my soldiers the order to kill upon contact. You will also allow us to leave here without disruptions and threats. From here on out, Anniah will take care of itself. Aparthia will no longer have any control over *my* nation. Do I make myself clear?"

"What if I say no? What if I refuse to relinquish control to you? What if I kill you right now?" At these words, the Royal Guard aims every weapon they have at the rebels standing before us, which I hadn't noticed until just now that Andrew and out of all people, Paul, are members of her crowd. I never thought I would see Paul again, so this is quite surprising to me. All three are so decked out in armor that it is hard to gain back the vision of them dressed as anything else.

"I suppose I should also mention that I have your sister, Princess Lily-Beth, contained in Anniah. If you do not meet my demands, I will give the members of the Renegade who are guarding her the order to kill her. If, on the other hand, you do as I have instructed, your sister will be released the second we are out of Aparthia's boundaries. You should weigh your options carefully, Prince David." I cannot believe the sight before me. I never knew Edith had a ruthless side of her. Seeing her now, I do not know how I ever had pity for her or felt she was weak. This woman is calculated, intelligent, and callous.

I divert my attention to David and can tell he is weighing his options. If he lets Edith and her Renegade, as they evidently call themselves, depart without issue, his sister will be safe, but if he doesn't let them go, he might not get this opportunity to diminish Edith and her posse again. I do not envy his current position.

"Give the order to release my sister. You have my word that we will not interfere with your exit from Aparthia."

"In good time, Prince David. First, I have to be sure you will not be trifling with us. Give your mother my regards. I am certain the coming days will be hard for her." Edith and her Renegade withdraw in unison. What a powerful sight they are.

A guard enters from the side, out of breath. "Prince David, it is your father. The blast we felt was detonated from inside his quarters. King Rennin is dead, sir. I am so sorry to be the one to tell you."

"What about my mother? Is she alright?"

"Your mother was in the bathroom, sir, so she has been taken to the medical wing for evaluation."

Everyone in the room is dismayed. How could this have happened? How was a bomb placed in the King's room without anyone noticing?

"Get out! I need everyone to leave!" David shouts. I attempt to reach for his hand, but think better of it when I see the look on his face - pure anger, not sadness.

When I near the library, doors open and I am pulled in. I spin around and deliver a hard blow into the chest of whoever has a hold of me. I hear a grunt and instantly recognize the man.

"Logan, what are you doing? What just happened?"

"I did it. I planted the bomb in the king's room. It is time for us to leave - now!"

Made in the USA
Coppell, TX
30 January 2020

15179045R00157